Fourth of July in Fiji

The Holiday Adventure Club Book Five

Stephanie Taylor

Chapter 1

June 21

St. Louis, MO

The mediation room was in a far-flung corner of the courthouse, and the air conditioning unit grumbled in protest against the sweltering humidity outside. Lucy was spending the first day of summer in St. Louis, stationed across a well-used wooden table from her ex-husband, Jason.

"And does your client acknowledge that, in fact, the deceased paid off the entirety of her student loans from medical school?" Jason's lawyer asked, looking at Lucy dubiously from over the top of a pair of squared-off reading glasses. His lawyer, Edna Hastings, had the kind of heavy bags under her eyes and the deeply etched lines ringing her lips that only came from years of smoking. A nicotine patch was visible on her upper arm through the silk of her pale blue shirt, and her hands shook slightly as she held a ballpoint pen between two fingers the same way she might have held a cigarette.

"Of course she's aware," Lucy's lawyer responded, his tone making it clear that the question was idiotic, at best. "Mrs. Landish had a warm and happy relationship with the late Ms. Landish, and therefore she is more than aware of the generosity that Ms. Landish displayed through the act of paying off the loans."

Mrs. Landish, Lucy thought, looking out the tall windows at the blue Missouri sky. *I don't want to be Mrs. Landish anymore...I haven't been Mrs. Landish in a long time.* She steepled her fingers together, elbows on the table as she gazed out at the green grass beyond the courthouse, watching as two men in business suits with their ties loosened walked over to sit beneath an old oak tree.

"In that case," Edna Hastings went on, "we think it's best that Mrs. Landish—"

"Please call me Lucy instead of Mrs. Landish," Lucy said, her attention pulled back sharply to the discussion going on at the table.

"Fine," Edna said firmly. "It would be in everyone's best interest if *Lucy* relinquished any holdings she has on the properties bequeathed to Mr. Landish."

Lucy's lawyer, a man old enough to be her father and with a belly as round as a basketball and a gray mustache that looked thick enough to sweep crumbs off the table after dinner, leaned back in his chair, an incredulous look on his face.

"Edna," Douglas Fortunato said, shaking his gray head. "You must be out of your mind."

"Is that your professional opinion, Doug?" Edna snapped back, rubbing the nicotine patch through the silk like that might hasten the delivery of the sweet nectar to her bloodstream. "Or are you just being an old crank?"

Mr. Fortunado slapped the table with his meaty hand, a gold pinky ring set with a rich red garnet hitting the wood loudly and causing Lucy to jump. "I would say that opinion is professional, Eddie," he said, using a nickname with her that caused her eyebrows to lurch skyward.

Even Lucy was at full-attention now. *Eddie?* Did her lawyer just refer to Jason's attorney by a nickname that sounded as if they'd played together on a softball team for elderly litigators? Was St. Louis home to some sort of bowling league for attorneys? Even Jason was sitting up straighter, watching Edna and Doug like a kid waiting to see which of his parents might snap first.

Edna stood up slowly, bringing herself to her full height of approximately five-foot-two inches. "Douglas Ransom Fortunato," she said, her eyes spitting fire. "Do not—I repeat *do not*—call me Eddie ever again. You know better."

Lucy watched, mouth open like a fish trying to breathe out of water, as her attorney stood up across the table from Edna, the tips of his fingers pressed to the wood. He pulled himself to *his* full height of approximately six-foot-four, breathing heavily as he stared her down across the table. They stayed like that for almost a full minute, neither looking away. Lucy watched Doug's profile and noticed that his mustache was twitching ever so slightly.

"I knew it," Edna finally said, her voice low and gravelly. "I knew it the day I met your mother."

"You knew *what* the day you met my mother?" Doug bellowed, making a fist and knocking on the table loudly for emphasis.

"That I should have never married you!"

Lucy's eyes flew to Jason's face; he looked as stunned as she felt.

"We've been divorced for nearly thirty years, you insane woman," Doug said, putting a hand to his forehead. "And you can leave my mother out of this, God rest her lovely soul."

Edna huffed. "Lovely? It's like you and I aren't even talking about the same woman." Edna picked up a small stack of files and straightened them, stuffing all the papers that pertained to *Landish v. Landish* into a cracked leather briefcase. "Jason," she said, turning to her client. "You have my apologies, and while we have to call a halt to this meeting today for what must be obvious personal reasons, I will reassign one of my associates to this matter and we will re-convene tomorrow. Same time, same place."

Jason blinked a few times, speechless.

"You have my apologies, Mrs. Landish," Edna said to Lucy, giving her a nod.

"She-devil," Douglas Fortunato said as Edna left the room. "You just never get away from your damned ex-wife," he said, shaking his head and shoving his own materials into an equally time-worn satchel. And then, as if realizing that he was saying this in front of a divorced couple at odds—the female half of which was actually *his* client—he had the good sense to look sheepish. "I'll reassign a different partner as well," he said. "I'm sorry for this, and we'll get you back on track tomorrow."

Fortunato beat a hasty retreat from the room, leaving Lucy and Jason sitting there as the AC unit clicked and buzzed in the window.

"Okay," Jason said, looking stunned. "I don't even know what we just witnessed."

"Our future," Lucy said wryly, standing up and pushing in her chair. She put the strap of her purse over one shoulder and smoothed the front of her skirt. "I'm guessing Doug couldn't keep it in his pants either."

"Lucy," Jason called after her, following her through the doorway.

Her heels clicked against the wooden floors of the old courthouse as she hurried toward the exit. There was nothing exciting holding her in St. Louis, but she did have a hotel room at a place with a decent pool, a stocked mini-bar, and free wifi, so she figured she could last another twenty-four hours.

She'd come back the next day and try again.

The next morning, Lucy stood outside the same mediation room, dressed this time in a floral dress that was belted at the waist. She had her hair swept into a bun and two-inch heels on her feet. It was hot and her legs were tanned from all the time she spent walking the beach in Florida, so she'd gone without nylons.

Right away, she caught Jason's new attorney staring at her bare calves and she cleared her throat to get his attention.

"Mrs. Landish," the young lawyer said, extending a hand and readjusting his gaze guiltily. "Axel Pleury."

"Please, call me Lucy," she said, shaking his hand as her own attorney approached. Douglas Fortunato's replacement was a much younger, greener lawyer with reddish hair and a shiny gold wedding band on his left hand.

"Nelson Bunch," he said, shaking both Lucy's hand and Axel Pleury's.

"I'm not late," Jason called, rushing down the hall with a blonde goddess on his heels. The woman held a toddler on her hip and looked harried.

Lucy's heart fell as quickly as her smile did; it was Giselle. The second Mrs. Landish. She hated to admit that she knew Giselle from an evening when she'd had too much wine and had looked her up on Facebook. That had been a low point, and an evening that she wanted to forget. In fact, she'd woken up the next morning, opened her laptop, and blocked Giselle's profile right away so that she would never again fall into that sad trap.

"Hi," Jason said, shaking hands with the new attorneys and introducing them to Giselle. Lucy watched it all, but for some reason she felt like she couldn't hear a word that was being said. Blood rushed in her ears and she felt faint.

"And this," Jason said, tugging at his earlobe—a sure indicator of how nervous he was, Lucy knew from experience, "is Lucy. Lucy, this is Giselle. And Max."

At his name, the towheaded toddler turned his head, looking at Lucy with big, blue eyes filled with wonder.

"It's nice to meet you," Lucy said, feeling her voice croak in her suddenly dry throat. She couldn't tear her eyes off of Max, even though Giselle's smooth-faced, thick-haired, New England beauty was nearly as compelling as the cherubic baby in her arms. *Baby*, Lucy thought in her head. *That was supposed to be my baby. My baby.* Her eyes went to Jason's face and she knew with one glance that he realized the perilous situation he'd put them all in by bringing his family.

"Hey, Giselle," Jason said, turning to his wife. "Why don't you and Max go play in the grass. There's no need for you to be in here on such a gorgeous day." At the word *play*, Max squirmed in his mother's arms, angling his body so that he could wiggle free and run off on his chubby little legs.

"Sure, honey," Giselle said, smiling at Jason with flushed cheeks.

Lucy couldn't tear her eyes off the three of them. They were gorgeous—like a family in a magazine. Giselle flipped her long, honeyed hair over one shoulder and shifted Max expertly to her other strong hip. Even Jason—a man she'd once loved and then felt such repulsion toward in the wake of his betrayal—even he looked sleek and handsome in the light that spilled through the tall courthouse windows.

Wordlessly, Jason leaned over and kissed Giselle on the lips and then mussed his son's hair. Giselle gave Lucy a small nod and smile and then walked back down the hallway, taking that beautiful baby with her.

"Well," Axel Pleury said, holding out a hand as the door to the mediation room swung open. "Shall we get on with this, folks?"

Jason gave Lucy the same look she'd seen on his face after he'd first admitted to her that he'd been having an affair with Giselle and that she was pregnant: one of contrition. Of guilt. Of apology. He looked like a Golden Retriever who'd been caught chewing an expensive leather slipper.

"Sorry," he whispered as Lucy brushed past him on her way into the mediation room.

You will be, Lucy thought, but the words stuck in her throat. It was too much, seeing Jason with the woman he'd left her for. Seeing them as parents to a precious baby when all Lucy had wanted for the last few years of her marriage was that very thing.

As the door closed behind them and negotiations began anew with two attorneys who—it seemed—had never been married to or divorced from one another, Lucy steeled herself for battle. No way would she allow Jason to take away her life, destroy their marriage, kill their chances at having a family together, and talk her out of the inheritance from Auntie Marion.

There was NO. WAY.

Chapter 2

June 24

Buffalo, NY

"So she was pretty?" Aunt Sharon asked, passing Lucy a dish of potato salad at the umbrellaed picnic table. She licked a bit of the salad from her thumb and frowned. "And she smiled at you? That girl's got some nerve."

"Yeah," Lucy said, taking the serving spoon and plopping a clump of potato salad onto her plate. Next to her, her mother was poking at a hamburger bun with her index finger. "She was very pretty, and she seemed a little nervous to meet me, I guess. Not as nervous as she should have been, though," Lucy added under her breath.

"Damn straight," Aunt Sharon said, picking up a napkin and reaching across the table to wipe a dab of ketchup off Lucy's mother's face. "Sit down, Yvette," she said. "Sit there next to Lucy and eat your burger, okay?"

Lucy turned to her mom and noticed that she'd put little finger-sized holes all over the top of the bun and scattered corn chips across the wooden table. "Mom," she said softly, "here you go." With quick, deft moves, she reorganized her mom's plate of food and scooted it closer to her.

"I can do this, Lucy. I can handle my own food," her mother said petulantly. "I'm fine."

Lucy exchanged a quick look with her aunt Sharon and then picked up her own burger with two hands, taking a big bite. It was clear that her mom was *not* fine, and that Sharon was getting rundown by the constant work that went in to being her older sister's primary caregiver. Now that Lucy was there for the second time in six weeks, she was able to better assess what kinds of changes her mother was undergoing, and to see how badly Sharon needed more assistance.

"Anyway," Lucy said, trying to finish the story. "We were able to sit down that second day and talk with both of our attorneys, but unfortunately we didn't come to an agreement. Jason and Giselle are hellbent on me signing over all three buildings, and there's no way I'm doing that."

A fat, lazy bumblebee hovered over the dish of watermelon chunks, and Lucy waved a hand over it to shoo the bee away. It had been hot and dry in Buffalo for so many weeks that the grass had gone brown. It crunched now under Lucy's feet as she kicked off her Birkenstocks and crossed her legs under the picnic table.

"So, let me get the details fixed in my old brain," Aunt Sharon said, setting an elbow on the table and holding up one hand. "That hilarious old gal Marion, Jason's great-aunt, she owned *buildings* in downtown St. Louis? And she didn't have any kids of her own?"

"That's right," Lucy said, setting her burger on the plate and picking up a chip. "She owned most of downtown, it sounds like, and no—no kids of her own. She and I were actually really fond of each other." She put the chip into her mouth and crunched it. "So when I heard she left buildings to me and Jason, I knew that she had a reason. Aunt Marion knew we were divorced. She didn't approve of how things went down between us, but she still kept Jason in the will."

"My favorite part," Aunt Sharon cackled, "is that she left you more of the property than she left him!" She hooted and slapped the

9

table with one hand. "That's just beautiful, if you ask me. Poetic justice."

"It does seem that way," Lucy agreed. She picked up her plastic fork and speared a chunk of watermelon from the bowl. "But now we're left with this mess of figuring out how to divvy it all up. He wants me to hand my portion over, and I want him to go take a long walk off a short pier."

"Fair enough," Aunt Sharon said, taking the bottle of ketchup gently from Yvette's hands before she squirted it all over her plate. Without comment, she relocated the ketchup and pointed at her sister's burger, indicating that she should take a bite.

"Well, we're not going to agree, so I guess we'll just keep haggling here for the time being." Lucy bit into the watermelon; juice dripped down her chin and she swiped it away. "But we really need to have some discussion about what's going on around here," she said, cutting her eyes in her mother's direction.

Aunt Sharon put her fingers to her lips and tipped her head toward the house, indicating that they'd talk about it later. It was clear to Lucy that her mother would most likely not pick up on what they were talking about, and this thought depressed her even more. This whole trip had been agonizing and so far had not provided her with any of the answers that she needed.

"So," Aunt Sharon said, wiggling her eyebrows and looking mischievous. "How are things with that cutie patootie, Nick?"

Lucy laughed. "Nick is great. He's offered to come up with me both times, but I really didn't want to tear him away from his business again. Besides, this trip started in St. Louis with the nonsense with Jason, so it seemed better to just go it alone."

"How about this next vacation tour you're going on, hon?" Aunt Sharon dished herself up more potato salad and then put a smaller scoop on Yvette's plate. "Fiji, is it?"

"Yes," Lucy said, sitting up straighter. She'd found during the first four trips of her round-the-world-in-a-year journey with the Holiday Adventure Club that these excursions were a source of pride for her.

So far, she'd managed to plan, orchestrate, and pull off trips with groups of tourists to Venice, St. Barts, Edinburgh, and Morocco, and now she was set to spend the Fourth of July in Fiji with a whole new group of people. "I'm pretty excited for this one. Someplace gorgeous and tropical."

Aunt Sharon looked at her dubiously. "Girlfriend, you live in Florida! Is that not gorgeous and tropical enough for you?"

Lucy laughed. "You'd be surprised how much a place starts to just be home, no matter how exotic it seems to other people. I'm really looking forward to going to the South Pacific. I've never been."

Aunt Sharon reached across the table once again to wipe something from her sister's chin, and as she did, the thick white strap of her bra slipped out from under her tank top. Lucy watched how patient and caring her Aunt Sharon was with Yvette, and in an instant, she knew she could never do what her aunt was doing. At least not without a certain measure of resentment. She lowered her head and looked into her lap, twisting her paper napkin between her fingers. How could she ever thank her aunt for taking charge when her mother's agoraphobia widened and morphed into a diagnosis of dementia? How could she ever show her gratitude to the woman who'd taken over for her in Buffalo and set her free? It had been a long road for Lucy following her divorce from Jason, and she knew in her heart that she'd never be as far along in the recovery process as she was if she'd been forced to stay in her hometown and run into her ex-husband and his new family all the time. Had she stayed at her job, doing autopsy after autopsy and then coming home to spoon-feed her mother...well, she couldn't have done it, that was the point. She couldn't have done it and survived.

When she looked up again, Aunt Sharon was watching her with a soft smile. "You okay, baby girl?"

Lucy nodded. "Yeah. I'm good. I'm just..." She looked around at the backyard of the house she'd grown up in. Next door, Mr. Eggerton still had a giant scarecrow standing guard over his tiny vegetable garden, and down the street, Heather Miller had bought her parents' house and was raising her four little girls there. She'd gone to high school with Lucy and made it a point to come by and say hello every time Lucy came to town. "I'm just really grateful to you, Aunt Sharon," she said. "Without you here, I couldn't have started my own business, or moved to Florida, or—"

Aunt Sharon reached across the table and this time, rather than doing something to help Yvette, she put her hand over Lucy's. "It's okay, honey. My sister needed me, and I'm old. I've had my fun. I got married and did some traveling, but now I'm perfectly okay being here. You, however, have years ahead of you to do all the fun stuff. You're seeing the world, and you've got a cute man down there in sunny Florida. I could try to lie and say I wasn't a little jealous, but more than that, I'm happy for you. This is the order of things, my love." She patted Lucy's hand and then sat up straight again, looking at all the food on the table. "Now what do you say we get this cleaned up and put your mom down for her afternoon nap? We've got stuff to talk about."

* * *

With the picnic all cleared up, the leftovers stored in the fridge, and the dishwasher humming in the kitchen, Lucy and Sharon sat together at the table under a loudly ticking wall clock.

"Your mom is hanging in here, girlfriend," Aunt Sharon said, folding her meaty arms and resting them on the table in front of her. "She has some good days and some bad ones, but overall, she's doing just fine."

"Seriously?" Of course it's what Lucy wanted to hear and what she desperately wanted to be true, as it would alleviate some of her own guilt at not being there full-time, but she really needed the truth.

"For the time being, we're managing things. We've got the alarms on all the doors and windows following the little bonfire out in the yard," she said, reaching out with a thumbnail and digging into a groove on the wooden table. "And, on occasion, your mom is fully aware of how much work she's making for other people. In fact, she apologizes for it sometimes."

Lucy's head snaps up. "She does?" In all the years that Lucy had been the main point-person for her mother's needs, she had never once apologized. Instead, it had always been, "Do you think I *want* to live like this, Lucy? Do you think this is *easy* for me?"

"She definitely does. Although I think she played up the helplessness when Nick was here," Aunt Sharon said with a wink. "She was very fond of him."

Lucy gave a half-hearted laugh. Was this true? Her mother was suddenly self-aware and apologetic? She wondered if this could possibly just be an effect of the dementia, if maybe her mother's personality had undergone some sort of shift due to the disease. It wouldn't be unheard of, as she knew full well that people suffering from dementia frequently became angry and belligerent, or just generally underwent changes that made them seem even more like strangers to their loved ones. But was that even a thing—did people actually become nicer and more self-aware with dementia?

"I'm pretty fond of Nick, too," Lucy said, reaching for the plastic napkin holder that was shaped like Betty Boop. She dragged it closer and absentmindedly straightened all the paper napkins, setting them in the holder again. "But I'm really thinking about this whole thing with Jason. If we can settle this issue between us—and I have no idea what that might look like—then I might have more money to work with. And the one thing I know about a progressive disease that requires an increase in the level of care is that it also requires an increase in the level of funds. So just know that I'm planning ahead for that."

The clock ticked loudly between them in the silence for a long minute.

"That would really be helpful, Lucy," Aunt Sharon said carefully. "But in the event that things don't work out that way, I just want you to know that I still have your uncle's life insurance socked away, and I'm willing to dip into that to help support my sister."

"Oh, god! Aunt Sharon—no!" Lucy nearly shouted. She caught herself when she remembered that her mom was sleeping just down the hall and dropped her voice. "I would never in a million years ask you to do that."

"You aren't asking, sweetheart, I'm offering. Yvette is my big sister, and this is my situation, too. You hear me?"

Lucy blew out a long breath. "I hear you, but that would be an absolute last resort for me. I'd move back home before I'd let you do that."

"Oh, *pshaw*," Aunt Sharon said, standing up from the table. "Like hell you will. You keep that sweet fanny down in Florida where you belong, and don't lose a wink of sleep over this—at least not now. We've got time." Sharon opened a cupboard and moved a vase to the side. She stood up on her tiptoes and reached back, pulling out a bottle of tequila. "Now, can I make you a little drink while your mother snoozes?"

Lucy laughed. "It's only three o'clock!" she protested, glancing at her Apple watch.

"Your point?" Aunt Sharon lifted an eyebrow, holding the tequila in one hand and a lime in the other. "You want a paloma, or no?"

"I had no idea you were a bartender."

"You have no idea how long life can feel when you're suddenly widowed at fifty. I needed a hobby, and mixing drinks seemed as good as any."

Lucy nodded. "Fair enough."

"And anyway," Sharon said, setting things on the counter and pulling out two glasses. "A paloma's got grapefruit juice in it, so it's basically like a smoothie."

At this, Lucy actually guffawed. "A smoothie? Is that how you sell yourself on an afternoon drink?" She got up from the table and went to fetch a few grapefruit from the fruit and vegetable drawer in the refrigerator. "Although I'm not saying you don't deserve it."

"I don't drink every afternoon! Please don't think that. Dear lord...your mother isn't driving me to drink or anything. Oh, Lucy—I don't want you thinking I'm not a fit caregiver!" Aunt Sharon actually looked horrified.

"No way," Lucy reassured her. "I wouldn't judge you if you did have a drink every afternoon while she napped. I know I would."

They worked in tandem to fix the drinks and then sat down at the table again. Aunt Sharon sighed as she held up her glass. "To you, Lucy, my darling. To the wild hair you got to turn your life upside down after that no-good ex-husband of yours turned it inside-out. You're a tough cookie, whether you think so or not."

"To tough women everywhere," Lucy said, clinking her glass against Aunt Sharon's.

"Now go and have a fabulous time in Fiji, and tell me all the gory details," Aunt Sharon said, taking a sip of her paloma. "And if you see any hot men in loincloths, I want pictures!"

Lucy felt the punch of tequila hit her almost immediately. "You got it, Aunt Sharon. There will pics of gorgeous men coming your way—you have my word."

They clinked glasses one more time and then drank until Yvette woke up from her nap.

Chapter 3

June 30

Fiji

The resort was set on a lush piece of property that felt like it existed separately from the rest of the world. Lucy walked the path between the bungalows she'd reserved for her guests and the pool area, carrying her sandals by the straps so that she could feel the sand under her feet.

She opened the gate to a giant infinity pool that blended seamlessly with the horizon and the water beyond. Rows of lounge chairs were lined up perfectly, and at one end of the pool, two women in yellow flower print sarongs stood with trays in their hands, talking to one another while a woman with a light meter took readings and shouted numbers at someone behind a video camera.

"We'll take this from the top again," the cameraman said, moving his equipment aside so that his face was visible. He wore a red baseball hat turned backwards, and his eyes were tired. "Let's have the two waitresses, walking along next to the pool, talking to one another," he shouted, kneeling on the concrete as he focused on the women in sarongs. "And...go!"

As Lucy stood at the gate watching, the two women started walking, smiling placidly at one another and talking quietly. Each had a bright pink hibiscus tucked behind one ear, and the one closest to the pool was so tanned and shiny that her skin looked like a smooth acorn. They were both gorgeous, and as they moved, two men with reflectors walked along, making sure that light was bouncing off of their dewy skin.

"Cut!" the cameraman called, standing up with some effort and rubbing his knees. "Anything for the shot, huh?" he said with a laugh, looking at the woman with the light meter. "Looked good to me."

"Next shot?" the woman asked, taking out a phone and scrolling through her notes.

"Can I help you?" one of the light reflector guys asked Lucy. He was smiling as he towered over her, his floppy, grown-out hair held back by a thin elastic headband.

"Hi—sorry." Lucy tucked her long hair behind her ear. "I didn't mean to get in the way."

The tall guy gave her a lopsided smile. "As long as you've signed a waiver, you're good to go," he said, giving her an awkward thumbs-up.

"Oh, I did," Lucy said, shifting her woven bag from one shoulder to the other and tossing her sandals into it. "My name is Lucy Landish, and I run a travel agency called the Holiday Adventure Club. One of my tour groups is arriving today, and we'll be staying for the week."

"Right on, right on," the guy said, nodding and looking more and more like a frat boy with every passing second. "I'm Todd, and this is the crew of *Wild Tropics*."

"I didn't know that you guys were filming for *Wild Tropics*!" Lucy said, her mouth falling open. "I loved that show!"

"Yeah, it was dope, right?" Todd nodded heartily. "I was still in college when the show first aired, but I watched every episode."

"That was shot on Christmas Key, right? In Florida?" Lucy asked, watching as the cameraman climbed up on a short step ladder and focused his lens on the mosaic tiled palm tree at the bottom of the pool.

"Definitely," Todd said, giving her another thumbs-up. "Cute girls in bikinis doing competitions on the beach—can't beat that."

Lucy laughed. "My thoughts exactly." She watched distractedly as the rest of the crew bustled around the pool deck, moving chairs and setting up umbrellas. "But is this the same set up? Are you doing another competition-type reality show?"

"Uhhhh," Todd said, looking around and then leaning in to Lucy and lowering his voice. "Totally on the DL, since I'm not really supposed to talk about it, but no. It's more of a dating thing this time around. We've got eight sexy singles here at the resort, and I think things are gonna get pretty spicy."

"Ohhhh, gotcha." Lucy winked at him knowingly. "I'll keep that under my hat."

"So you should pretty much just carry on however you normally would while we're filming," Todd went on, glancing at the watch on his wrist as it buzzed with a message. "We're not looking for our contestants to have an isolated experience here, and we want to capture the story of the whole resort while we're following our potential love matches around."

"So we actually get to be *in* the show?" Lucy clasped her hands together. "I might get to be on *Wild Tropics*?"

"Welllll," Todd said, tipping his head from side to side, "you might show up in a scene at the pool or something. Unless the producers ask you for something more specific."

"Wow, okay." Lucy looked around again. Suddenly the pool felt like a glamorous movie set. "I was just thinking we might accidentally get caught in the crosshairs or something. I wasn't thinking that we were actually going to be a part of it."

Todd shrugged. "Yeah. Pretty much anyone who stays here and signs the release is fair game. So watch yourself!" He wagged a finger at her and laughed. "I'd hate for you to show up on *Wild Tropics* and have all your dirty laundry aired for the whole world to see!" He cackled—somewhat maniacally, Lucy thought—and then carried his light reflector over to where the cameraman was angling his shot into the pool.

Lucy continued to watch for another minute or two before letting herself back out through the pool gate. She wandered on, admiring the tropical foliage and the lazy river that ran beneath the wooden footbridge as she crossed over it. Beneath her, two teenage boys floated on rafts down the lazy river, legs dangling over the yellow plastic boats and into the chlorinated water.

"*Bula!*" one of them called up to her, waving a hand as he drifted by, disappearing around a bend and out of view.

"*Bula!*" Lucy called to his friend, who waved back. She'd already learned *bula*—which meant *hello*, or *welcome* in Fijian, as well as the phrases for *please* and *thank you*. Aside from Fijian, Hindi was a common language in the country, as was English.

On the long plane ride that passed through Sydney, Lucy had read up on the history of the island nation and its surrounding areas. The South Pacific had always appealed to her, and now that she was there, she realized that she'd been right to feel the pull of Fiji. The salty ocean air; the fragrant floral scent that drifted on each breeze; the way everyone had the faint glimmer of a relaxed smile on their faces—this was truly paradise. It put Florida's hot pavement, ticky-tacky souvenir shops, and the gaudy putt-putt golf courses that seemed to exist in every beach town to shame.

At the main building, which housed the lobby, concierge, the fine dining restaurant, a gift shop, and the spa, Lucy pulled her sandals from her bag and slipped them back onto her feet. She walked through the sliding glass doors and right into a Polynesian retreat. The dark wood floors and counters were rich and smooth beneath the high, peaked ceiling which looked like a thatched roof. Beams lashed with rope ran through the center of the open air above, and from them, dark bamboo ceiling fans hung, spinning slowly to keep the air circulating. Every resort employee was dressed in a variation of the yellow sarongs that Lucy had seen on the servers by the pool, with the men in yellow button-up shirts made from the same fabric, and the women in skirts, dresses, or flowing pants of the same pattern.

"Good afternoon," a stunning, dark-haired woman said, smiling at Lucy. She stood behind the counter, hands folded as she waited for Lucy to approach. "*Bula.* Welcome to The Frangipani Fiji. How can I help you?"

"Hi, I'm Lucy—"

A sudden commotion behind Lucy interrupted her words and she turned toward the sliding doors, along with everyone else in the lobby, in time to see a woman with two giant Great Danes on leashes. They pulled excitedly on their leather leads, wrapping themselves around the woman and toppling the cart next to her that was loaded with matching Louis Vuitton luggage.

"Bridger! Bagley!" the woman called out, spinning around and trying to untangle herself, but only ending up more twisted in the process. "Halt! Sit! Now!"

Lucy had turned her back to the counter and to the beautiful woman who had greeted her, and so she didn't even notice when the woman slipped out from behind the counter and rushed forward to try and control the hurricane of fur and luggage.

"Oh!" the woman holding the leashes called out, stepping over an expensive-looking duffel bag that looked big enough to hold a body. "This is *not* how we wanted to make our entrance, boys!"

Lucy felt a half-smile tugging at her lips as she watched the woman scold her dogs like they were mischievous toddlers. When the woman finally righted herself with the assistance of the desk clerk, who had pulled the luggage out of the way and expertly re-stacked it on the cart, she exhaled, straightened her shoulders, and plastered a big smile on her face.

"Well," she said, sweeping her hair off both shoulders and straightening her flowing maxi-dress, "that was quite a scene." One of the bellhops moved in and took the leashes from her hands, freeing her up to glide toward the front desk unencumbered. "Hi," she said in a sweet voice, sidling up to the front counter and standing next to

Lucy. She took a purse from her shoulder that looked to Lucy like it must have cost at least one of her monthly mortgage payments and dropped it onto the counter with a sigh. "I can't believe I finally made it!"

Lucy smiled at her. "Looks like you came with your hands full."

The woman put her elbows on the counter and leaned her head into her hands, running her fingers through her expertly highlighted hair. On her fingers were several of the biggest, clearest diamonds Lucy had ever seen, and on one wrist were no fewer than eight tennis bracelets, dazzling and glinting in the light.

"Oh, I did come with my hands full, but I wasn't going to leave my boys home alone for a week—I couldn't," she said breathlessly, turning to Lucy. "Now that my kids are grown, Bridge and Bags are my babies. Do you have pets? Or kids—maybe you have kids," she said, her thoughts running together as she spoke rapidly.

"I have a cat," Lucy said.

The woman nodded, but Lucy could tell that she wasn't really listening.

"I'm Mindy Shultz," the woman said, thrusting a diamond encrusted hand at Lucy. "I'm here on vacation with my dogs, hoping to find some sort of spiritual connection to nature, or to the water. I don't know. I just know I needed to *not* be in New York City in July with both of my ex-husbands crawling around."

Lucy shook Mindy's hand. "I hear that one thousand percent."

Mindy laughed. "Okay, so even though you don't have dogs, I take it you feel me on the ex-husband bit."

"I do. And I sympathize. I'm Lucy Landish, owner of the Holiday Adv—"

"Oh my god! Lucy!" Mindy threw her arms wide and wrapped Lucy in a tight embrace. "I'm so glad to finally meet you. I feel like we talked at least a thousand times leading up to this trip."

"Maybe three or four times," Lucy said with a smile, "but we did put in a lot of work getting things lined up, didn't we?"

Mindy let go of her and took a step back, looking Lucy up and down. "You're just gorgeous, you know that?"

"Oh, thank you," Lucy said, looking at her feet to hide the blush creeping up her cheeks. She wasn't great with compliments, and had never gotten used to overly effusive displays from people. So many years working in the calm quiet of an autopsy room had acclimated Lucy to working around people with patient hands, keen observation skills, and the ability to complete tasks in relative silence. Oh, and the people on her tables never said much either.

"I'm sorry I didn't mention Bridger and Bagley coming along, but I was really anticipating that my son Michael would be home to watch them. He, however, had entirely different plans." Mindy waved a hand through the air and the wide sleeves of her long caftan dress trailed behind her arm.

In Lucy's opinion, Mindy seemed like a perfect example of boho chic. But rich boho—definitely someone who paid a lot to look like she caravanned around the country and went glamping in perfectly appointed tents filled with candles and linens from Anthropologie.

"As long as it's okay with the resort, it's okay with me," Lucy said, turning back to the front desk to find that the lovely woman who'd done nothing more than introduce herself to Lucy before Mindy had blown through the doors was back, standing there with an expectant smile.

"Mrs. Shultz called us in advance," the woman said, folding her hands benevolently. "It's all been arranged."

"Oh god, thank you," Mindy said, bowing her head as she reached across the desk and took the woman's hand in hers. She squinted at her name tag. "Jasmine. Thank you."

"Not a problem at all."

Mindy turned back to Lucy. "I landed at the airport and came right over. Am I early? Late?"

"Just on time," Lucy said, watching as Jasmine checked Mindy in efficiently, making her key cards and motioning for the bellhops to snap to attention and get the dogs and luggage sorted. "I just met the film crew out at the pool, and as long as you've signed your waiver for your stay here, then you don't need to worry about them at all."

"Oh, you *did* email us all about that," Mindy said, accepting the key card that Jasmine slid across the counter to her. "I signed my waiver, and I am SO EXCITED to be on *Wild Tropics*. You have no idea!" Her laugh tinkled like windchimes. "I hope the cameras catch me frolicking on the beach with an extremely hot younger man," she went on. "I want both of my ex-husbands to eat their damn hearts out when they see it."

Lucy couldn't argue with that line of thinking. "Well, they did say that the cameras were following life at the resort as well as the people who are on the show, which apparently is more skewed toward dating or a love match or something this time."

"No physical challenges? No competitions?" Mindy asked, looking disappointed.

"I don't think so."

"Mrs. Shultz?" Jasmine interrupted gently. "Dean will show you to your bungalow," she said, gesturing at an earnest looking young man with his hair swept back off his face and fixed firmly with far too much gel.

Mindy tossed her hair behind her shoulders again. "Actually, it's Ms. Shultz—I went back to my maiden name after the debacle that was my last divorce," she said, turning to Lucy. "Huge mistake. Won't make that one again!"

"Well, I'm glad you're here," Lucy said, her words trailing behind Mindy as she followed young Dean back through the sliding glass doors. A second bellhop was close behind them with Bridger and Bagley tugging at their leashes to reach their mistress.

"Me too!" Mindy called with a wave. The sun outside lit up her diamonds like sparklers as she slipped on a pair of Oliver Peoples sunglasses and let the bellhops lead her to her home away from home.

Chapter 4

June 30

Fiji

Mindy Shultz sat at the foot of her bed, looking out of the open end of her bungalow at the crystal clear blue water beyond. This trip to Fiji had been something spontaneous that she'd wanted to do for herself; this was her first big voyage out into the vast world without a husband by her side, and she wanted to get it right.

Kevin had been who her parents expected her to marry. In her day, a girl went to college to either pick an honest, servile career as a teacher or a nurse, or to find her future husband. It had been no mystery to Mindy as she'd sat in economics classes and daydreamed about babies and decorating a vacation house whether or not she was there to learn how to be a kindergarten teacher—she most definitely *was not.*

So she'd gone to frat parties with Kevin, wore his letterman's jacket, and gone home to meet his parents at Thanksgiving, winning them over almost instantly with the fact that she was the sole heiress to the Shulnuts fortune, which had been built on her great-grandma Betsy's recipe for a simple cake donut. From there, the following generations had taken the donuts wide, adding crullers, fritters, danish, scones, and popovers to the menu, and eventually stocking every single domestic flight in America for every airline, the entire line of Hilton hotels, and the pastry cases of over 12,000 Shulnuts shops around the country. But it was when Mindy's father had the idea to partner with Capra's Coffee to turn what had been simple bakery storefronts into real sit-down coffee shops that things had gone off the charts. Mindy was sitting on something like four hundred million dollars in holdings and stock options, and that simple number blew her mind. She could hardly even comprehend it.

Her money had also far surpassed Kevin's family's impressive but more sedate fortune, and that had really stuck in Kevin's craw. In order to reestablish his alpha-ness in the relationship (at least according to his therapist, as reported to Mindy by her ex-husband himself), he'd gone outside the marriage to "seek validation and self-fulfillment." Mindy had called B.S. on that and used a tiny bit of her money to send Kevin on his merry way to keep finding validation elsewhere.

She stared at the turquoise water, remembering that time just after her first divorce. She'd been forty-five and suddenly free after more than twenty years, but still with three teenagers to finish raising. Had she done that right? She didn't know—did anyone really know? And certainly now she was left questioning some of her methods and motives. Michael was thirty and a freelance technical writer who dated widely and prolifically with men he met on a dating app. Shayla was twenty-four and working for some kind of organization that helped the homeless population of New York City (Mindy was proud, mind you, but the organization wasn't one that she recognized from her philanthropic enterprises or from her connections, so she wasn't entirely sure that Shayla was working for a reputable non-profit. And of course she would have preferred that Shayla be doing such work as a means to personal growth while a successful husband brought in the money, and not to pay her bills, but that was terribly out of vogue these days, so Mindy kept her mouth shut on that one).

And then there was Emory. Stubborn, twenty-one year old

Emory. She'd taken her parents' divorce the hardest, as babies often do, and had fallen into partying and a life of glamour and luxury. Her current enterprise was something she called "social media influencer," but which sounded to Mindy like non-stop gallivanting around the world with a camera in tow. And when she forced herself to click through her youngest child's Instagram and to watch her TikToks, it was all she could do not to cringe at the way Emory appeared to be nothing more than a porcelain, vacant-eyed girl with money. Her video snippets from yachts moored in Ibiza, from the top of the Eiffel Tower at night, and on private planes with people who looked like models did not impress Mindy. She wanted more for her children. She wanted them all to find their footing and be self-reliant and grateful humans. She wanted them to live lives that she could be proud of—that *they* could be proud of.

With a sigh, Mindy got up from the bed and walked out to the deck that stretched across the entire front of her bungalow. A tiny plunge pool was positioned to one side with two chaise lounges nearby, and Bagley and Bridger had made themselves at home there, heads on front paws as they eyed the water and the horizon beyond. Mindy flung herself onto one of the chaises and put an arm over her eyes dramatically. This was a beautiful place, and she'd chosen the very best time of year to visit: virtually no rain, and temperatures in the low 80s. It was picturesque—like a glossy magazine spread right before her eyes—but for that moment, she couldn't stand to look at it.

Because after Kevin there had been Arthur. Her biggest mistake. The one thing she regretted as a woman and as a mother. It stung to think of it now, but she forced herself to say the words out loud, even though no one could hear them: "I married my ex-husband's brother." *Uggghhhh*, Mindy thought, cringing to herself. She'd actually done that. She'd allowed some sort of revenge fantasy to play out whereby she let Kevin's younger brother flirt with her at a booze-soaked summer party in the Hamptons. When she'd woken up the next morning in his arms she'd known it was a mistake (how could it *not* be?), but instead of admitting that to herself in the bright light of morning, she'd accepted a few dates with him back in the city, which led to her convincing herself that she'd simply been married to the wrong brother all along, which led to a tasteful ceremony in Central Park and a very distasteful divorce six months later. God! She'd married her *children's uncle*. And not just that, but he was eleven years her junior. The way she'd embarrassed her kids and herself was humiliating to look back on now. It certainly didn't warrant the way her kids treated her like a nutcase or a loose cannon, but deep down she couldn't blame them for not having approved.

Mindy hadn't realized that she'd drifted off until Bagley nudged her hand with his cold nose.

"Hey, buddy," she said, using both hands to push herself into a sitting position. Her head was foggy and thick with the feeling of an unexpected catnap. She rubbed her hands over her face, careful not to wipe off her eye makeup. "You doing okay?"

Bagley sat on his haunches and watched her curiously. Had she truly brought the dogs along because Michael was unavailable to watch them, or were they her de facto companions? The answer was fairly obvious to her, but Mindy wanted to keep believing that she'd packed them onto her private jet and brought them to Fiji entirely out of love and care and not because, at fifty-four, she'd realized that her best and most reliable friends were dogs.

"Let's go for a walk, huh?" she said, standing up and clapping for them to follow, which they did, wagging their tails excitedly.

Outside her door was a long wooden walkway that wound through twenty-four bungalows over the water. It looked like the kind of screensaver that people put on their computers at work so that they could daydream about being in paradise instead of at their jobs. Each separate unit had its own deck with a mini pool, and they were set at angles to provide maximum privacy from one another. Mindy wandered down the dock with Bridger and Bagley, nodding and smiling at people as they set themselves up on their own chaise lounges or stood in the opening of their sliding doors, admiring what looked like endless miles of clear blue water.

At the end of the walkway, Mindy wound one leather leash around each hand, warning her boys to heel and behave as she stepped onto the main property. A group of six teenagers tossed a football around on the thick, green grass, looking like an ad for Abercrombie & Fitch. Mindy watched them for a second, remembering her own kids at that age. Utterly self-conscious and self-critical and yet totally beautiful at the same time. Ah, youth.

She walked on, passing a camera crew as they set up a shot at an outdoor bar area.

"Hi," Mindy called, waving at a young woman wearing a sun visor and aviator shades. "Are you shooting soon?"

The woman stopped what she was doing and looked at Mindy as if she were some sort of oddity. Perhaps people didn't stop and just interject themselves into the show like that? When the woman didn't answer, Mindy smiled and walked on.

She chose a sandy path beyond the main building and followed it down to a private beach. Beneath a clump of palm trees stood a wooden shack with a hand-painted sign that said "Surf & Stuff." Mindy tied Bridger and Bagley to a tree and walked in.

"*Bula*," said a man without a shirt. He had his back to Mindy and from where she stood in the doorway of the small shack she could see his muscles rippling beneath his tanned skin. On the bicep of his right arm was a band of tribal tattoos, and his hair was a rich brown that had been lightened by the sun. When he turned to face her, the palest blue eyes she'd ever seen looked out at her from above sharp cheekbones. "Can I help you?"

Mindy looked around: surfboards; kayaks; sunscreen; beach towels.

"Is this all for rent?" she asked.

"Pretty much," the man said, one corner of his mouth quirking up in a smile. "The surfboards and kayaks are for rent. The towels and sunscreen are yours if you buy them."

"Well," Mindy said, walking around barefoot on the sandy floor of the shack. "I don't know how to surf or kayak, so maybe I should just buy some sunscreen." She picked up a spray can of SPF 50 and pretended to read the label while her eyes trailed up the back of the man's smooth, hairless legs. In fact, every inch of skin that she could see was smooth and hair-free. It made his muscles even more visible.

With an even bigger smile, the man lifted up a surfboard and placed it on the rough wood counter where his register sat. "This one seems right for you," he said, watching her with amusement.

"Again, I don't know how to surf," she said, feeling his eyes burn into her as he watched her pick up and set down several more cans of sunscreen.

"Lucky for you, I give lessons."

Mindy looked at him. "Oh?"

Instead of speaking, he gave her a single nod and patted the surfboard on the counter.

"How much for everything?" she asked, though naturally she didn't care what the cost was. It just seemed that people expected you to need to know before making any sort of a commitment.

He tipped his head to one side and squinted like he was deep in thought. "How about two hundred dollars for eight lessons and the surfboard rental?"

Mindy looked around; she wasn't sure if this was his personal business or part of the resort. "Am I expected to bargain?" she asked, cocking her head just like he'd done.

"You're expected to show up here tomorrow morning at seven o'clock for your first lesson. Wear a swimsuit."

Mindy blinked a few times. She wasn't used to A) men this good looking, and B) having someone cut through the bull and just say it like it was. "I'll be here," she said, turning and walking out the door and back into the afternoon sun.

She untied Bridger and Bagley and walked down onto the beach with one leash in each hand. *Huh*, she thought, watching the way the sun sparkled on the South Pacific as she felt the sand beneath her feet. *I guess I'm going to learn to surf.*

Chapter 5

June 30

Fiji

"So, what are we thinking so far?" Heinrich Nilsson asked his crew. They'd put all their equipment safely out of the way and sat down at the round tables under the open-air bar, ready to eat sandwiches and nachos and to talk about what came next.

"I liked that shot this morning," Todd said, putting his reflector, which had been folded and zipped into a black carrying case, on an empty chair nearby. "The one of the women walking by the pool."

A waitress in a sarong swept by and left a stack of menus on their table. Everything for the duration of their stay was being comped by the resort in exchange for the publicity the show would bring, but Heinrich had already warned his young crew that this did *not* mean it was okay to run up enormous tabs at the resort's five bars.

"This is feeling pretty commercial to me," Spencer said, picking up a menu. She was the girl in the sun visor and aviators to whom Mindy had attempted to speak, and she didn't appear overly impressed with either the guests at the resort or with the angle of this season's *Wild Tropics*. Her attitude normally wouldn't go over well for someone with her job title, which was Assistant Production Coordinator, but her close and extremely personal relationship with Heinrich Nilsson, the director of *Wild Tropics*, gave her more leeway than the others had. Heinrich knew that and at times made an effort to mitigate the obviousness of his favoritism, but at other times—like now—he was simply hungry and tired and just wanted to appease her so that he could eat something.

"It is a bit commercial, Spence," Heinrich said, looking at his own menu and using the tone that a patient father might use with a bored teenage daughter. "But that's between the network and the resort, right? We're just here to make compelling TV."

"I guess," Spencer said, inspecting her cuticles. "I just wish we could exercise some creative integrity when it comes to deciding whether to film Avon and Pietro fighting drunkenly by the pool at night, versus getting to know the real guests here. I would be willing to bet that their stories are a thousand times more interesting than the wannabe actors we chose for this season."

Heinrich lowered his menu and gave Spencer a look of dark warning. "Creative integrity is for documentaries about endangered species, Spencer. And I'm not creeping around and filming Avon as she uses her outdoor shower in the morning, I'm simply documenting the real ups and downs that people go through as they forge relationships in an unnatural setting."

Todd breathed in and held it as he looked back and forth between Spencer and Heinrich, as did everyone else at the surrounding tables.

"Is it really not possible for us to pitch it to the network and see if we can't get this show to focus more on real people and their real lives?" Spencer picked up her water glass and drank, pulling out an ice cube with her teeth and crunching it loudly.

"They really want to capitalize on the success of the other reality shows that put young singles together in far-flung locations and see what happens. I know it's not necessarily up to the high standards that a girl who went to Yale might hold, but for a good portion of the viewing population, it's wildly entertaining."

Spencer pushed her chair back and stood up. "Then maybe we

need to re-think the strategy of pandering to the lowest common denominator and instead introduce them to something more high-brow. I'm not hungry." She grabbed her miniature backpack and slung it over one shoulder before walking away as she studiously avoided Heinrich's gaze.

Everyone busied themselves with their menus and with sipping water, eyebrows raised questioningly at one another during fleeting glances. Spencer had already established herself as the outspoken one of the group, the opinionated rich girl who had lowered herself to be an assistant as a path to paying her dues on the way to the top. But there were moments where her attitude and insubordination toward Heinrich made the rest of them wonder how and why she hadn't been fired and shipped back home already.

For his part, Heinrich actually felt more relaxed with her gone. He pulled a pair of reading glasses from his crossbody bag and slipped them on, realizing as he did that he'd carefully packed away little things like needing glasses around his younger girlfriend. As he sat there perusing the menu, he also relaxed his stomach muscles, feeling the middle-aged paunch loosen and his body settle into repose. He'd been about to order a salad, but without Spencer there to quietly assess him, he decided on a burger. With fries. Extra fries. And maybe a beer.

"We ready to order?" he asked the rest of the group with a huge smile.

Todd took off that damned headband he always wore to hold back his ridiculous floppy hair. *Why don't men just act like men anymore?* Heinrich thought, eyeing the motley group of Millennials that made up his crew. *Why don't they get decent haircuts and why in the hell do they polish their damn nails?* He eyeballed Drake's fingers, which were covered in a chipped electric blue polish. Maybe it was being over fifty, or maybe it was just the relaxing of societal norms that had happened too late to have any real effect on him, but Heinrich couldn't entirely wrap his heads around these kids.

Take Spencer: she was clearly attracted to him (why, he wasn't sure), and at times she could act wildly mature and dazzle him with her Ivy League education and worldliness, but at other times, she could throw these little tantrums and put their relationship on full, glaring display by pushing the limits of what she could and should be saying to him. He sighed, watching her cut across the resort, her figure growing smaller in the distance.

"I'm hella ready to order," Todd said, putting his bony elbows on the table. "I'm getting nachos and a burger. How about you guys?"

Heinrich looked at the menu through his bifocals, holding it out and pulling it closer again until he could read the print that no one else at the table seemed to be struggling with. "I'm having a burger and onion rings," he decided, slapping the menu down on the table and glancing at Spencer's now empty chair. "And a margarita."

* * *

A young woman wearing a visor and aviator sunglasses waved at Lucy as they approached a short footbridge from opposite ends.

Lucy had just watched Mindy Shultz and her dogs roll into the resort and then she'd made a few arrangements with the concierge before setting off to explore a bit more.

"Hi," the woman said, taking off her sunglasses as she and Lucy walked toward one another at the center of the bridge. "Are you the owner of the travel agency with the big group staying here?"

Lucy smiled, though she had no idea who this girl was. "I am. I'm Lucy Landish with the Holiday Adventure Club."

"Spencer Clark, from *Wild Tropics*." Spencer leaned her elbow on the railing of the footbridge and looked at Lucy. "I was hoping I'd run into you."

"Well, here we are," Lucy said, nodding and wondering why exactly Spencer had been hoping to meet her. "I'm excited to be on the island while you guys are filming. I'm a fan."

Spencer gave her a half-smile. "For sure." She narrowed her eyes.

"And what I'm wondering is whether you have anything you think would make for good tv. Like, do you have a story?"

Lucy laughed and put a hand to her chest. "Do *I* have a story?" Her eyebrows shot up. "I don't think I do. My life is pretty boring."

"No way. Everyone has a story. You married?"

"Uh," Lucy said, taking a step back. "Divorced."

"So maybe you'll meet someone here at the resort?" Spencer leaned onto her elbow and gave Lucy a long, searching look.

"Wait," Lucy said, waving her hands in front of her. "Time out. I've got someone back home in Florida, so no to that, and why do you care about my story? What's going on?"

Spencer craned her neck and looked at the lazy river that ran under the bridge. There was no one floating down it at the moment, but the water rushed and hit the rocks along the sides as it flowed.

"Okay, Lucy, I'm gonna be straight with you. I think this resort is full of people with really good, fascinating stories, and I think we're missing it. Our network wants us to focus on this dating angle where we bring all these oiled-up gym rats to a resort and then film them as they lust after one another, but I don't think that's the right direction."

Lucy listened, taking it all in. "Okay," she said. "And you are...the producer?" she guessed.

"Not technically." Spencer stood up straight and looked Lucy in the eye. "I'm more of a production coordinator, but I'm trying to pitch a stronger angle to our director. He's got more pull with the network than I do, obviously. I mean, I'm twenty-six. It's not like anyone is going to listen to a girl who's only been out of college for a few years."

"Riiiggghhht," Lucy said, nodding. "Okay. I see what you're going for. And I'm sorry to disappoint you, but I don't know that I'm personally anyone worth following around and making a documentary about—"

"You might be," Spencer interrupted. "You don't know. But what about your guests? Anyone in your travel group who might prove interesting?"

A vision of Mindy Shultz and her dogs instantly filled her mind. The woman *did* seem fascinating, and from the brief conversations that Lucy had had with her before the trip, she knew that Mindy was heiress to the Shulnuts fortune. But no way was she about to give up personal information about one of her group members to this woman who had basically accosted her on the bridge looking for dirt.

"I'm afraid I don't know much about them yet," Lucy said. "I'm sorry. Most of them are arriving this afternoon, so once they get here I suppose you can talk to them personally and see if anyone is interested in helping you develop your storylines."

Spencer unzipped a crossbody purse and pulled out a business card. "Here," she said, handing it to Lucy. "That's my cell. Call or text anytime, day or night. I really want to find something amazing, even if I have to do all the legwork myself."

Lucy looked at the white business card in her hand. "Okay, I'll keep it in mind," she said, smiling at Spencer. "Good luck."

As Lucy walked on, she could feel Spencer standing in the same spot on the bridge, assessing her as she watched her go.

Chapter 6

July 1

Fiji

Seven o'clock in the morning. The air was still cool and fresh, and the grounds of the resort were peaceful. As Mindy rushed from the bungalow in her bikini covered by a pair of white running shorts and a tank top, she waved at a gardener who was picking fallen leaves from a flowerbed with his AirPods in, head bobbing along to the music.

She'd agreed to meet an extremely hot stranger for a surfing lesson, and she could actually *hear* her daughter Emory's voice in her head: "*Mom,* seriously. Surfing is for young people. And you probably remind that hot guy of his mom or something." (Insert a million Gen Z eye rolls here as her daughter processed the idea that her mother would be *literally* getting on a surfboard in a bikini—SO. MORTIFYING.)

As Mindy chose the sandy path that had led her down to the beach shack the day before, she could feel her pulse quicken. Was it the fact that she was about to get a hands-on lesson from a man whose body and demeanor made him seem like a tough, mysterious hero in an action movie? Or was it that she was actually just nervous to wipe out on a surfboard? Even after years of yoga, pilates, running, and working with a trainer, Mindy was more than aware that her fifty-four-year-old body might not behave and respond the same way that it would have at thirty-four. She sucked in a breath as she rounded the bend to the beach shack and spotted Mr. Action Hero bent over a surfboard in the sand, waxing it with methodical strokes like a man saying a prayer.

"Good morning," Mindy said, walking up to him and hoping that the morning light wasn't too harsh on her un-made-up face.

He turned his head and smiled up at her from his spot on the sand. "Good morning. Conditions are perfect for us today."

"Oh good. Can I help?" Mindy stood next to him as he waxed, watching the muscles in his biceps ripple while he worked.

"You helped by showing up," he said evenly, not breaking his concentration again.

Mindy gave a little huff of a laugh. "You didn't think I would?"

This made him pause his waxing strokes, but only for a moment. "You'd be surprised."

"Are you saying that women are flighty?" Mindy felt her haunches go up and she tried hard not to feel affronted.

"No," he said gently, not sounding the least bit ruffled. "I'm saying *people* are flighty. They say one thing and then do another."

"Not me," Mindy said with conviction. "I might do the wrong things sometimes, but I finish what I start, and I do whatever I say I'll do."

"Then we have much in common," he said, standing and turning to face her. He was easily six-foot-two, and on closer inspection, Mindy could see that he wasn't ridiculously younger than her, but he was incredibly fit and most likely stuck to an uber-healthy lifestyle full of quinoa and water and avocados or something. "I'm Kona."

Mindy blinked. "Like the coffee?"

A small smile quirked Kona's mouth on one side. "Like the Irish name. My father is Fijian and my mother was Irish."

"I'm Mindy," she said. "Which is kind of a silly name for a woman my age. It's short for Melinda, which no one ever calls me except my grandmother, who is still alive, if you can believe that. She refuses to call me Mindy because she says it makes me sound like an overgrown cheerleader, but—"

Kona closed his eyes and didn't open them, which made the verbal lava that flowed out of Mindy's volcano of a mouth come to a halt.

"I think Mindy sounds like *windy,* and there's nothing more beautiful than the wind," Kona said, opening his blue eyes again and fixing them on Mindy's face.

His eyes. Clear and icy like blue topaz. Mindy was transfixed. But his proclamation about the beauty of the wind made her do a tiny internal cringe. Because seriously, that line would have *never* played in New York City. A guy in a bar telling her that her name sounded like the beautiful wind? *Ugh.* But somehow, weirdly, as he stood there smiling at her with absolutely no guile, she melted a little. So far he seemed entirely like the kind of guy who said exactly what he felt, so why would this be any different? Maybe he was a middle-aged man who truly loved the wind?

"Okay," Mindy said with a smile, swallowing the fear that was once again rising in her and pushing upward through her ribcage. "So how do we start this adventure? Do I pay you? Can I just charge it to my bungalow? I brought cash just in case," she said, reaching under her tank top and pulling two hundred dollar bills from beneath the fabric of her bikini. To her embarrassment, she realized that it was still warm from being tucked in next to her breast.

Kona looked at the money and a shadow passed over his face. "I don't really care about that too much," he said. "I only said it would cost you to find out whether you were serious about learning to surf or not."

"Please," Mindy said, still holding out the hot hundred dollar bills. "Take it. You're about to earn it trying to teach a woman from

Manhattan how to surf." Her laugh was genuine as she waited for him to accept the payment.

He hesitated for another long moment before taking the money. "Okay, if you insist. Let me put this inside the surf shack." Kona had to duck his head slightly to walk into the shop and his broad shoulders nearly filled up the doorway, which made him look like a grown-up trying to get into a kids' playhouse.

Mindy swallowed again. Now she was absolutely sure: it wasn't just the surfing that was making her nervous. It was a pair of crystal blue geyser eyes. It was being close to a man who wasn't a boring stockbroker with a pedigree. It was being alone on a nearly empty beach with someone who could pick her up off the ground and carry her away like a feather.

It was Kona.

"Mindy," Kona said, emerging from the shack and closing the door behind him. "Let's get you in the water." He tossed her a wetsuit, which she slung over one arm as he picked up the surfboard.

She followed him down the rest of the path to the open beach, where he made a beeline for the water. For the first time in a long time, Mindy was there for it—every bit of it. She didn't worry about her grown children, her ex-husbands, or what any of her society friends would say about her jumping into the waves and the unknown. Instead, she followed along with a huge smile on her face.

But what she didn't see—what she couldn't have known—was that Spencer Clark was hiding out beside the beach shack, obscured by the bushes, her handheld camera trained on the morning sun, the waves, Kona's chiseled body, and at the woman who was peeling off her tank top as she walked, leaving it in the sand behind her.

Spencer was about to get some beautiful footage.

* * *

Heinrich watched from where he stood as Spencer and Todd put their heads together and discussed something that looked serious. It was hard for him not to put too much energy into wondering what it was, and it was definitely a challenge not to let his mind wander too far down the rabbit hole. Todd was a better match for Spencer, after all, and it was entirely possible that he was making inroads with her right under Heinrich's nose. But he needed to focus. He steeled himself and tried to listen to what was going on around him.

"And if we could just get Avon to talk about what she expects in a long-term relationship, then it would really help the audience believe that Pietro is a perfect match for her," one of the associate producers was saying on a FaceTime call that they were all huddled around. "We're loving the dailies that you're sending our way, and if we could just steer things a tiny bit in that direction, we think that would really help with editing things on our end."

The magic of technology made things so much easier for Heinrich. Not having the entire crew on location was a blessing in so many ways, and being able to send off what they'd gotten on a given day and wake up to feedback from home base was really helpful.

But what were Spencer and Todd doing now? Heinrich watched as they wandered off together, Spencer making hand gestures and talking to Todd with an earnest look on her pretty face. And sweet fancy Moses, was she ever pretty. Heinrich looked at her with longing, admiring the way her nose turned up just slightly in profile, and the way her pink lips pulled back to reveal perfect white teeth. She was a runner, and in the sun, her skin was smooth and pulled over taut muscles. Heinrich couldn't lie to himself: her youthful beauty had reeled him in, but it was her mind and her love of a challenge that had kept him. He'd never known a woman—of any age—so sure of herself and so driven by her own ideas and desires. She was mesmerizing.

"So, Heinrich, is that a go?" the producer asked, her face looking out at him from the iPad screen as she pulled him back to the task at hand.

"Yeah, yeah," he said absentmindedly, still watching Todd and Spencer as they walked away. "That's a go. Got it." But he didn't have it; at least, not entirely. What he had was a jealous itch that he needed to scratch. He'd confront Spencer later about whatever it was that was going on with her and Todd.

* * *

Spencer was counting on the fact that Todd had been brazenly flirting with her for the past six months as confirmation that he'd do whatever she wanted. The fact that he'd never get to cash in on whatever favors he sent her way wasn't a concern of hers at the moment.

"So then you'll help me?" she asked, stopping under a palm tree right in the center of the resort's wide, open lawn. "I'm going to need not just your assistance, but also your secrecy, okay?"

Todd nodded eagerly; he was such a Golden Retriever. Of course Spencer was flattered by his single-minded devotion as he'd fetched her drinks from the bar every night, or listened to her talk about her senior thesis at Yale, but he was no match for her. She would never waste her time on even the most perfunctory date with a boy when she far preferred the company of men.

"I'm all yours," Todd said, and the look in his eyes told Spencer that he meant it in more ways than one.

"Perfect. Then I'll need you to constantly be my eyes and ears around this place. We need to scout for people, locations, situations, romance, intrigue—anything. It can be staff, guests...doesn't matter. I just want some real, raw footage that builds a story. I don't even care if the people are stumbling out of their bungalows hungover, I just don't want to see a single twenty-three-year-old actress with her hair sprayed into beachy waves, or a monosyllabic male model ogling her as he high-fives another cardboard cutout of a man. Am I clear?"

Todd nodded excitedly. "Totally," he said. "Real people. Real stories. But how are we going to get this to replace what we've already got going?"

"We're not," Spencer said with a sly smile. "I have another idea entirely. But that's for later. I just needed to know that you were on my side, and that you'd help me and keep it all under wraps."

"God, Spence, yeah—of course," Todd promised. "You have my word."

Spencer stuck out a hand there under the palm tree and gave him a hard look in the eyes. He shook her hand and she gave it a single, firm pump. "Good. Then let's get to work."

Chapter 7

July 2

Fiji

"You wouldn't believe this weather, Nick. It's so beautiful here," Lucy said, flipping around the camera on her iPhone so that he could see the entire resort as she held up her phone and turned in a slow circle. "I'll send more pictures."

"I'm jealous," Nick said, smiling at her face as she turned the camera back around so that they were looking at one another. "What are you doing now?"

Lucy chewed on her lip as her mind raced ahead of her. "I've got a group of guests who want to go to the Garden of the Sleeping Giant and see the orchids, so we're doing that this morning." She glanced at her watch to check the time. "I'm meeting them here at the main building in about fifteen minutes."

"Sounds cool," Nick said, running a hand through his hair.

It was only about four o'clock in the afternoon back home, so Nick was behind the counter at The Carrier Pigeon, wrapping up his work day while Lucy was drinking the last of her coffee and looking ahead to a whole new day, given the fact that Fiji was sixteen hours ahead of the east coast. The time difference on this trip was making it somewhat easier for them to talk, but it still threw Lucy for a loop every time she realized that they were existing in different days.

"So what are you up to this evening?" Lucy asked, watching him as his eyes flicked to the windows of the shop. He lifted a hand and waved at someone who was walking by.

"I'm probably going to take Hemmie to the beach and maybe hit the bookstore. I'm not gonna lie; I'm lonely as hell without you." And from the look on his face as he gazed into the camera, Lucy knew he wasn't lying. "I don't know how we lived as just work-adjacent buddies for so long, because now when I'm not with you, all I'm thinking of is when I get to see you again."

"Hey, me too," Lucy said softly, watching him and feeling a twinge of sadness at the fact that they'd finally started something right when she was planning to travel the world. Her timing couldn't have been less conducive to a fledgling relationship, and she did feel some guilt about that.

"Oh, in other news," Nick said, shifting gears expertly so that the mood of their call didn't plummet to the ground floor. He was great at that: making sure Lucy never felt down on account of something he'd done or said. She marveled at it and frequently took lessons from Nick's easy way of just being. "I heard from Honey that your coffee buddy is gonna be out for a while."

Lucy frowned. "Dev?" It rankled her just the tiniest bit that Nick would refer to him as her "coffee buddy" and not simply by his name, but she let that go. "What do you mean?"

Nick shrugged. "I've been making my own thermos of coffee at home and bringing it with me, so I haven't been in for a while, but Honey said his parents were running the shop, and that neither of them was very forthcoming about where he was."

"Do you think he's sick?" Lucy could hear the note of panic in her own voice, and she worked quickly to tamp it down. "He's probably just taking a break. Everyone needs one, right?"

Nick nodded, but his face made it clear that he was sitting on a few words he wasn't quite prepared to say. Instead, he made eye contact with Lucy and smiled. "You never get a break though. Maybe you need one, too."

"I get to vacation all around the world!" she said, taking a drink of the coffee in the to go cup that she'd wrangled from the breakfast buffet. "This is enough of a break for me. And I was basically off there for the six weeks after my trip to Morocco."

"Come on, Lucy," Nick scoffed. "No one would consider those six weeks a real break for you. All you did was plan for this trip, go back and forth to Buffalo to check on your mom, and deal with your ex-husband."

"And his new wife," Lucy added for good measure. "Don't forget that part, which was a real treat."

Nick made a sympathetic face. "See? You work your butt off all the time, whether it's for the travel agency or to keep things moving ahead in your personal life. All I'm saying is that you deserve a vacation."

Lucy raised her coffee cup toward her phone like she was raising it in a toast. "Hear, hear!"

"I was thinking," Nick went on, nodding at someone who had walked into his shop and dropping his voice. "Maybe when this year is over and you've done your final trip, we can get away somewhere— just the two of us. No travel groups, no distractions. What do you think?"

Lucy was stunned that a man was willing to plan a vacation with her six months into the future. She made a face like she was pondering the idea and nodded enthusiastically. "Wow. Yeah," she said, taking the last sip of her coffee and tossing it into the outdoor garbage can next to her. "That would be amazing to do something that wasn't in any way work related. Seriously."

"Okay, then it's a date. For next January," Nick laughed. "But for now, I have Mrs. Aisley in here to mail a package overseas to her grandson, don't I, Mrs. Aisley?" he asked, speaking louder for the old woman who Lucy already knew was hard of hearing.

"Who is that?" Mrs. Aisley asked, pointing at the phone as Nick flipped the camera to face her.

"Hi, Mrs. Aisley!" Lucy said loudly. "It's Lucy Landish. I'm in Fiji."

Nick did a quick screen flip and then turned the phone itself around so that Lucy and Mrs. Aisley were looking at one another.

"Oh, it's that skinny girlfriend of yours," Mrs. Aisley said, pointing at the phone. "The one with the tiny bosoms."

Lucy laughed on her end as Nick guffawed on his. "Mrs. Aisley!" he said. "I would prefer you didn't comment on my girlfriend's bosoms."

"Well, no one else is going to," Mrs. Aisley said, sounding salty at being reprimanded by Nick.

"I'll let you two handle your business there," Lucy said, still laughing. It didn't bother her one bit that Mrs. Aisley felt free to comment on her figure. She'd spent enough time around older women to know that their filters tended to go on the fritz around age seventy, and she was absolutely sure that, if she'd wanted to, Mrs. Aisley could have come up with something far worse than calling her skinny and flat-chested.

"Sorry," Nick said, turning the phone back to his own face and grimacing. "I better deal with this."

Lucy laughed softly and blew him a kiss with her fingertips, but in the background she could hear Mrs. Aisley wondering loudly why Nick felt he had to apologize to a girl whose ta-tas were the size of bee stings.

They ended the call just as the first members of the group walked up to Lucy. So far, everyone seemed easygoing and there for a good time. At the mixer on the first night, Lucy had realized she had a few people who were ready to drink their way through the stay on Fiji, which of course was fine with her—their money, their choice—and a few others who were completely enamored of the culture and the flora and fauna, so she was totally in her element. She'd planned a few things that would hopefully make everyone happy, starting with the trip today to the Garden of the Sleeping Giant, which boasted over 2,000 different types of orchids, all tucked into a lush jungle setting with wooden walkways and thick greenery.

The resort provided them with a chartered bus to the gardens, and once there, they took a quick introductory tour with a guide and then went their separate ways to enjoy the grounds. Sometimes on trips Lucy ended up hanging out with a few of the guests, and other times she wandered solo, and this time she found herself alone and walking through bursts of the most beautiful orchids she'd ever seen.

Truth be told, she didn't mind being on her own for this one, and as she stopped to take photos with her phone of the various blooms of orchids, she thought about Nick and the little life they were carving out together back home. Since their trip to St. Barts in March, they'd become inseparable. Of course she'd always known that Nick was a stand-up, what-you-see-is-what-you-get kind of guy, but he'd solidified that by being her rock through her trips so far, and also by flying up to Buffalo to check on her mom and help her aunt. She knew that wasn't the kind of thing that just any guy would do, and the ease with which Nick drifted through life, reading books and walking his dog, suited her just fine after the tumultuous end to her marriage and the nonsensical pseudo-relationship she'd gotten into when she'd first moved to Amelia Island. Nick was everything she wanted.

Correction—Nick was everything she *should* want. But was it all too easy? Where was the heart-pounding, lust-inducing fever that marked the start of most relationships? Was it okay that they'd so quickly slipped right into life as an old married couple? They understood each other's pasts and honored the lives they'd had before they met each other, but if she was being honest with herself, there was no real fire in Lucy's heart when it came to Nick. She cared about him, she loved his company, she appreciated his sense of humor, and she enjoyed being his girlfriend, but on her subsequent trips following the start of their real relationship (to Edinburgh and to Morocco) she had missed him, but she hadn't *missed* him.

She got on her knees in front of a burst of hot pink orchids with overly pronounced yellow stamens, angling her camera to capture the spray of darker spots across the petals of the flower. As she did, she thought about the Instagram posts she'd make on her Holiday Adventure Club account, highlighting the trip and showcasing the resort, which had given her a really nice group discount. Ramping up her social media presence had been at the behest of Dev, after all, and he hadn't steered her wrong so far with his business advice. In all honesty, his guidance had really lit a fire under the first couple of trips, and with some simple tweaks to her approach, he'd shown her how to really market her business—at least on a small scale.

And Dev—where *was* he? She hoped he was alright. He'd never once had anyone fill in for him at the coffee shop, and while they hadn't spoken again about anything personal after he'd walked through the door of her travel agency following her trip to Morocco, he hadn't indicated that a leave of absence was on the horizon when she'd gone next door for her coffee on most work days. The person who would know what was up was Honey Joplin, owner of the nail salon in their strip mall and self-appointed Queen of Gossip for all of Amelia Island. But a phone call to Honey from 7,000 miles away to ask where Dev was seemed totally out of bounds, so she tucked the thought away and moved on to take some photos of the vegetation that lined the weathered wooden walkway.

At the moment, none of it mattered, nor could she do anything about it, so she vowed to put it all away and just enjoy Fiji. She'd found on her journeys thus far that the best thing about them was the way her real life became almost like some fictional story; whenever she wanted, she could shut the book and put it away for later.

Almost.

Chapter 8

July 2
Fiji

Mindy stood beneath an outdoor shower that was tucked around the side of her bungalow and shielded from view by a swinging wooden door. She turned her face to the sky, eyes closed, and let the soapy water run through her hair, then down her bare back, thighs, and calves. She turned her body around and opened her eyes to look at the ocean beyond her shower. The side of the enclosure that faced the sea was wide open so that the person in the shower could see the water. Of course, if someone happened to boat or swim by, then who knew—maybe they'd get a free show. But for those not interested in potentially flashing passersby, there was always the indoor shower.

Mindy turned off the water and pulled her towel down from where she'd slung it over the wooden door. She buried her face in the soft fabric and inhaled, unable to hold back a smile and a little squeal of joy. She'd done it! She'd surfed. Okay, only for a few seconds, but she'd gotten herself upright on the board with Kona's help, and had held her pose for several beats before being knocked unceremoni-ously into the water. It felt amazing—exhilarating, really—to have done something she'd never done before, and to have done it with someone whose entire demeanor was calm, patient, and gentle.

She wrapped the towel around her body and walked across the front of her deck, passing the dogs as they lounged in the sun. Mindy stopped and bent over, holding her towel closed, so that she could give each of her boys a pat on the head. She'd employed young Dean the bellhop for the duration of her stay to be her personal dog walker (with his boss's permission, of course) and he was being paid a king's ransom to show up three times a day and walk the boys while Mindy went about enjoying the resort without having to dash back to her bungalow mid-meal or leave the pool in a hurry to walk the dogs.

The walk-in closet opened to reveal far more clothes than Mindy would ever wear on one vacation, but she was a woman who liked options. She'd packed basically the entire portion of her closet that housed her resort wear, and now she selected a sheer linen dress in a sumptuous tangerine color to show off the light tan she'd already started to develop. It hit her mid-calf, and the thick shoulder straps were looped through a wide hem so that it cinched like a paperbag around her collarbone, tying jauntily on one shoulder with an over-sized bow. For her feet, she chose a pair of gold gladiator sandals that laced up over her ankles, and for her ears, a pair of thick, matte gold hoops.

Once dressed, Mindy walked into the bathroom and flipped on the makeup mirror. She had work to do. Not as much as at home, mind you, as the sun and the relaxing feeling of being on vacation had done wonders for the bags under her eyes and for her coloring, but still. A woman of a certain age always put on a dab of concealer, a swipe of mascara, and some bronzer and lipgloss.

Mindy recapped her mascara as her phone started to vibrate on the counter. She glanced at the screen: it was Shayla, her middle child.

"Baby, hi!" Mindy said, propping her phone up so that she and Shayla could see one another while they FaceTimed. "How are you?"

"Hey, Mom," Shayla said, her voice muffled slightly by the traffic, construction noises, beeping of trucks, and the general hubbub of New York City. "Sorry, I'm headed to Brooklyn for dinner, so I thought I'd call you. Is this too noisy?"

"No, honey, you're fine. I'm so happy to see you!" Mindy forgot about her makeup entirely and instead gazed at her daughter's smooth, unmade-up face. Her undoubtedly messy hair was covered with a scarf like a chic 70s mom, and a tangle of studs and tiny chains rimmed her earlobes. Much to Mindy's dismay, Shayla also had several tattoos marring her perfect skin, but that wasn't something Mindy liked to think about. In her day, a young lady of a certain social status wouldn't have even considered permanently inking flowers on her body, she would have just bought a nice floral dress from Laura Ashley and gotten on with it. But times had changed, and while Mindy didn't always agree with the things her kids did, she tried her hardest to adapt and to at least not comment on the things she disapproved of.

Shayla looked away from the phone as she checked both ways before crossing the street. "I'm just leaving work here," she said, the image of her bobbing slightly as she walked. "I've been managing a fundraiser that we're doing in October, and it's my job to drum up some leads to solicit, or to sell tickets to, and I was hoping I could talk to you about—" (*Oh no, here it comes*, Mindy thought) "getting ahold of your address book and sending out invites to the people you know who might be potential donors." (*Ugh. There it was.*)

"I see," Mindy said carefully, reaching for her gold powder case and snapping it open so that she had something to do with her hands. "Well, that's lovely, sweetheart. I'm so proud of you that you're running a fundraiser. There's so much to learn in the world of philanthropy!" *How to say no...how to say no...* "It's just that giving away one's personal contacts to a random charity is kind of frowned upon. It's like a company selling your personal information to another company without your permission—"

"Mom," Shayla interrupted her, frowning at the screen as she stood on a street corner waiting for the light to change. People flowed around her on the hot pavement and Mindy could see the late afternoon sun on her daughter's bare shoulders. "You're not selling anyone's personal information to some random charity or company. You'd be helping your own child to get a leg up at work. And what do you care about these people anyway? Are they your actual friends? I doubt it. When you and Dad split up, did they call and offer to take you out?"

"Some of them did!" Mindy said defensively, snapping her powder case shut again with a loud click. "Heather Jones-Morris did. Andrea and Dave Wurtzler invited me to their beach house, and—"

"Mom," Shayla said, sounding serious. "Listen to yourself. 'Doug and Mary Snootzleheimer-Wagbush invited me to high tea.' It's ridiculous. These people are *not* your friends. Sharing their information with me is how this whole thing works."

Mindy gave a hard laugh. "How *what* whole thing works, Shay?"

Shayla made an incredulous face. "Charity. Society. New York. Come on, Mom. You've lived this life for like a million years."

"So flattering, Shayla."

"You know what I mean. You think in all these years that Heather Jones-Morris never passed on your contact information to the Organization for Longer-lasting Gel Manicures or whatever?"

Mindy inhaled and exhaled. Now her daughter was just being spiteful. "Honey," she said, keeping her voice level. "I'm just saying it's not something that I'm personally comfortable with."

Shayla nodded, her mouth pressed into a tight line. "Okay. Fine. I hear you, Mom. You think my job is a joke and therefore you won't help me in any way. You'll pat me on the head and pretend you think I'm doing good things for the world, but you won't put yourself out there in any way to really give me a leg up at work."

A man wearing a unicorn head passed behind Shayla and appeared on the screen; no one around her even gave a second glance. Mindy loved New York.

She focused on her daughter's angry face once again. "Shayla, it's not like that at all."

"Whatever, Mom. Have a great time in Fiji. I'm sure you're down there doing great things for the world," she added, her words laced with sarcasm.

"Shay," Mindy begged, ready to try to help her daughter understand her position. But Shayla had already ended the call and the screen went black. She set the phone on the counter softly and looked at her reflection in the mirror once more. What she saw there was a woman who'd been through it all in the past decade. Just a series of ups and downs, failures and losses, embarrassments and fresh starts. And it showed—if not on her face, then in her eyes. And she wanted to find herself again, to be the Mindy Shultz she'd been all the years of her life when money and status weren't something she'd had to consider on a daily basis.

As she looked at her face in the mirror, Mindy realized that the road to authenticity and wholeness was hers alone to find. No amount of big city dating, charity work, or gold star mothering of her three adult children would fill the hole in her heart that had grown over the years as she melted into the mold of Upper East Side Society Mom with Money, but some real work on herself and some intense soul-searching might do the trick. *Maybe I'm not down here doing great things for the world,* Mindy thought as she ran a hand over her still-damp hair, *but I am down here trying to do some positive things for me.*

* * *

The first positive thing Mindy wanted to do was to start losing some of her baggage. Some of the literal *stuff* that she carried around. To that end, she walked into the main building, found the well-appointed ladies' restroom with its hushed lounge area that led into the marble-floored, highly-polished bathrooms. She closed herself into one of the stalls and when she came out, the attendant, who was dressed from head to toe in white, was busy folding and re-stacking the laundered hand towels. The attendant had wordlessly set a towel on the counter for Mindy, then gone back to her task.

After Mindy washed her hands and dried them on the towel, she quickly unclasped one of her diamond tennis bracelets and set it in the dish meant for tips. By the time the attendant turned and glanced in her direction, she'd already slipped out the door.

Back outside, she wandered the grounds, meandering in and out of different areas with different-sized bungalows. There was also a series of buildings that housed eight units apiece, and these were clearly the rooms that were more hotel-like than private residence-like. A maid's cart was paused outside one of the open doors, and through it, Mindy could see a young woman in a uniform with a white apron bent over, vacuuming beneath a bed. Her hair was wet along the hairline from exertion, and as she worked, Mindy could see a small, determined smile on her face.

The door to the next room was open and it was completely bare—stripped of sheets and linens with no luggage visible—obviously in the midst of being turned over for new guests. Mindy ducked into it and walked straight over to the desk. Inside the single drawer she found a notepad, a pen, and an envelope, all embossed with the words *The Frangipani Fiji*. Mindy clicked the ballpoint pen and wrote: **For you. A tip and a token of gratitude for your hard work. Do with it what you will!**

She quickly folded the note and stuffed it into the envelope, then slid the diamond pinky ring she'd gotten from Kevin (the *first* time he'd cheated) off her finger and dropped it into the envelope. Mindy saw no one watching, so she walked out of the room stealthily and dropped the envelope onto the young maid's cart, making sure it was positioned atop a pile of towels where she'd see it.

Mindy was nearly to the sandy path that led to Kona's shack on the beach when she started to get the distinct impression that she was being followed. She slowed her gait and then paused at a bloom of flowers on a shrub, pretending to admire them. Looking one way and then the other, she spotted the young woman from the film crew, looking down at the screen of a handheld video camera. She was wearing her sun visor again, but had her aviator sunglasses off and was gazing intently at whatever footage she'd gotten.

Mindy turned and started walking in her direction. "Excuse me!" she called out, waving at the woman. "Hi there!"

Spencer looked up, her eyes widening in surprise. "Hi," she said hesitantly.

"Well," Mindy said, shrugging her lightly bronzed shoulders, "we *are* in Fiji."

"True, true," Spencer agreed, turning off her screen and holding the small camera at her side.

Mindy walked closer. "So, are you getting some extra footage of the resort to fill in the planned shots?" She nodded at Spencer's camera.

"Yeah, something like that."

"I'm Mindy Shultz," she said, smiling expectantly at Spencer. "And you are?"

"Spencer, from *Wild Tropics*."

"I see," Mindy said, appraising her. "You look terribly familiar. Are you from New York?"

Spencer nodded, looking oddly guilty. "I am," she said, glancing away for a long minute. "My parents are Genevieve and Macon Clark."

"Oh my god! Honey!" Mindy put a hand to her chest and her mouth dropped in shock. "Genevieve and I go *way* back. That's incredible! How are your parents?"

Spencer smiled half-heartedly. "They're good. Probably in East Hampton right now getting ready for their annual Fourth of July bash."

"Yes!" Mindy cried, laughing. "I've been to their party a time or two." Once, at the Clark's Independence Day shindig, she'd even caught Kevin with his hand up the skirt of a girl who couldn't have been much older than their son, Michael.

"Their parties are legendary," Spencer agreed, looking suddenly less like a television studio exec and more like the daughter of Mindy's moneyed friends.

"So tell me," Mindy said, leaning in like they were co-conspirators, "what's going on with the dating show?"

Spencer made a thinking face. "Ummm, welllll...it's pretty much par for the course, you know? Attractive young people in a gorgeous setting, flirting and shmoozing for the cameras."

Mindy's face fell. "That's too bad. It seems like there must be other exciting things going on around here. Like, maybe the staff has an interesting story. In fact, I'm sure they do. Imagine it: people working hard to take care of their families, going through their own dramas while they put on pleasant faces to wait on all of us. There could be something there."

"You're so right, Mrs. Shultz. I wholeheartedly agree that there are more interesting things happening at The Frangipani Fiji than what we're officially getting on film."

Mindy reached out and took Spencer's hand in hers, holding it for a moment. "I knew you'd understand, Spencer. You're a Yale girl, am I right?"

"You are correct," Spencer said, giving a single nod.

"Then maybe it's just a matter of putting in your time on a show that's not your cup of tea, and before you know it you'll be doing the work that's in your heart. You'll see."

"I wish I had your strong conviction, Mrs. Shultz," Spencer said.

"Please—Mindy." She squeezed Spencer's hand and then let it go. "What a treat running into Genevieve and Macon's daughter all this way from home," she said, shaking her head as she marveled at the coincidence. "Keep your eyes peeled for interesting things going on around here—I bet you'll find some ideas of your own that go beyond what the network is pushing for!"

Mindy gave a little wave and walked on, turning toward the main building so that she could make a few spa appointments instead of wandering back to see Kona for the second time in one day. After all, it wouldn't do to be overly eager. And Kona was really just her surf instructor—nothing more.

"Don't you worry, Mindy," Spencer said under her breath as she hurriedly turned her camera back on and pointed it toward her mother's friend. "I'm finding things that are far more interesting than what the network wants us to film."

She already had a nice shot of Mindy sneaking out and leaving something on the maid's cart outside the empty hotel room, and now she wanted a little more footage of Mindy's retreating figure, the sunlight playing through the thin, linen fabric of her tangerine sundress as she walked across the perfectly cut grass.

Chapter 9

July 3

Fiji

It was way too early when Lucy heard a knocking at the front door of her bungalow. She'd spent the evening before with about ten of the travelers in her group, singing karaoke and knocking back tropical cocktails at the open air bar by the beach, and by the time they'd finished, she'd laughed her way back to her bungalow with a happy buzz, escorted by a husband and wife from Rhode Island who had come on the trip to do a vow renewal ceremony by the sea.

She rolled over in her giant, comfortable bed, not pulling her sleep mask from over her eyes. Maybe the knocking was just in her head. Or maybe it was housekeeping and they'd realize they were much too early, because she was pretty sure she'd managed to put the Do Not Disturb sign out before falling into her bed still wearing the purple satin slip dress she'd worn to karaoke.

But the knocking persisted, and finally Lucy swung her legs around and shoved her sleep mask up into her hair. She looked around: the curtains were wide open to the stunning display of sky and water beyond her little deck, and the first thing she wanted to do was brew a coffee in her bungalow's Keurig machine and go sit out there on the lounge chair, letting the ocean breeze and the morning sun wake her up slowly.

Instead, she tried to straighten out the straps of her slip dress, pulling one from where it had fallen and putting it back in place. Beneath the dress she still wore a bra, and with the dress askew, a patch of black lace was visible. She kicked her sandals out of the way and picked up her purse, which she'd dropped on the floor just inside the doorway.

Lucy put a palm flat on the door and leaned against it for a long second as the knocking continued.

"Lucy?" a man's voice called out.

It jolted her into the present. That gravelly voice. The timbre of it. The way her name sounded. She reached for the handle and pulled open the door, forgetting that she had a sleep mask on top of her head and most likely pools of mascara from the night before still smudged beneath her eyes.

Lucy sucked in a breath and held it; her heart hammered in her chest.

There, standing outside her bungalow on the wooden walkway in Fiji, over seven thousand miles from home, was Dev Lopez. He held a worn duffel in one hand, and he lifted the other in a tentative greeting.

"Good morning," he said, smiling at her with amusement. "Catch you at a bad time?"

Lucy squinted in the bright morning light and stepped back so that the sun wasn't in her eyes. "Dev," she said, yanking the sleep mask off her head. "What are you doing here?"

He shrugged and glanced left and right. "I was in the neighborhood?"

Lucy felt as though this was supposed to amuse her, but instead it only served to frustrate her. "I thought you were sick or something."

Dev frowned. "Why would you think that? Do I look sick?"

Lucy's sigh sounded angry—almost hostile. "No, I just...never mind. I'm trying to wake up here. I'm really confused. Can I please get dressed and meet you in the restaurant for coffee?' She looked at the bag in his hands. "Wait, are you staying here? With me?"

Dev laughed and held up a hand. "What? No! I wouldn't show up here and presume to sleep in your bungalow. I have my own," he said, gesturing to the left. "Two doors down."

Lucy had so many questions, but she didn't want her mouth to get ahead of her slow moving brain, so she took a deep, cleansing breath and exhaled. "Okay. Then give me thirty minutes, please, and let's meet in the restaurant that's adjacent to the main lobby. They serve brunch till noon."

Dev looked at his watch. "Better light a fire then, Miss Adventure," he said with a smirk. "Because it's already 11:15."

* * *

Lucy walked into the restaurant twenty minutes later with her wet hair pulled up into a braid and sunglasses covering her clean, makeup-free face. She found Dev at a table on the patio, where the glass doors were open to make the whole place flow into one giant indoor-outdoor restaurant.

"You'd better hit the buffet before it closes," Dev said, raising his coffee cup. He already had a plate loaded with bacon, scrambled eggs, fresh fruit, and breakfast potatoes, and a carafe of coffee sat on the center of the table.

Lucy shoved her sunglasses onto her head and made a quick trip through the buffet line, grabbing a croissant with jam and butter, a poached egg, and a little plate of different cheeses. It was more than she'd normally eat first thing in the morning, but then this wasn't first thing in the morning, and she didn't normally wake up wondering whether she'd had three, or four Mai Tais.

"Okay," Lucy said on a sigh, setting her plates down, pulling out her chair, putting her sunglasses back on her face, and sitting down all in one fluid motion. "Talk." She reached for her coffee mug, which was still turned upside down on its saucer, then filled it to the brim with hot, dark coffee.

"I could beat around the bush here, Lucy. Or I could make dry jokes, which I'm pretty good at, but I'm going to be honest with you, which is what I was trying to do when I brought you that coffee in your office and told you that I should have spoken up sooner."

Lucy drank her coffee like it was water, then set the cup back on its saucer and poured in a bit of cream. "The caffeine is coming," she said, stirring the cream into her coffee with a spoon. "But I'm not fully tracking yet."

Dev put his coffee down and leaned forward with a serious look on his face. Lucy had no choice but to do the same.

"I should have told you sooner that I think you're an amazing woman, and that I wanted to take you out. Get to know you better. See if there was something there." His hazel eyes searched her face, though she knew her sunglasses were blocking the eye contact that he wanted from her.

Lucy looked around at the people sitting closest to them. She leaned forward in her seat and dropped her voice. "So you got your parents to watch the coffee shop and you flew all the way to Fiji to tell me that you should have tried to date me?"

Dev sat back, looking suspicious. "How did you know about my parents?"

"Come on, Dev. Amelia Island is a tiny little universe of its own. Honey mentioned it." She ripped a piece off of her croissant and smeared it with butter and jam before putting it in her mouth.

Dev's eyes narrowed. "You've talked to Honey since you've been in Fiji?"

Lucy chewed slowly, taking her time. While she swallowed, she reached for a fork to pick up a piece of cheese from her plate. "Not exactly."

"Then how did you hear that? Wait," Dev said, a slow smile spreading across his face. "Did you hear that from Nick? Are you two talking about me?"

Lucy nearly choked on the hard cheddar she'd bitten into. "He just mentioned that Honey said something about you being gone, and I drew my own conclusions. It's nothing."

"Hmm. Okay." Dev watched her from across the table. "Then I won't assume that Epperson is jealous of me in any way, nor will I draw any conclusions about your interest in my whereabouts."

Lucy set her coffee cup down with a clatter and took off her sunglasses, lack of makeup be damned. She looked Dev directly in the eye. "You can draw whatever conclusions you want, Dev, but frankly I'm still stunned that you're here. You actually left your business in someone else's hands, flew halfway around the world, and showed up on the doorstep of my bungalow without warning. This is either the most insane or the most romantic thing a man has ever done for me."

"More romantic than Nick following you to St. Barts?"

Lucy rolled her eyes impatiently. "He didn't follow me, I invited him. And that's where our relationship took a turn."

"I see," Dev said, watching her get flustered. "Then it's safe to assume that a man who's willing to travel to a tropical place for you might also be a man you're willing to have romantic feelings for?"

Lucy wasn't sure whether she should feel flattered or outraged, though she was quickly leaning toward the latter. "So, you think that I'm some kind of dim-witted floozy who sleeps with whatever man is willing to travel for me?"

"God! No, Lucy," Dev said, backing up slightly in his chair. "Maybe you and I should just take a breather here. I could probably use a nap after all that travel, and you could probably stand to fully wake up after whatever happened to you last night." He couldn't fully stifle a grin here. "I'm not trying to insult you in any way, and I kind of feel like my explanation for why I'm here is taking a weird path. Can we just start again later on?"

Lucy picked up her coffee with shaky hands. "That's probably a good idea. Because right now I'm feeling like you're the kind of man who would swoop in and try to steal another man's lady, and up until this point, I really thought you had more self-restraint than that."

Dev looked guilty. "I'd like to think I had more self-restraint too, but you've never been in my shoes, Lucy." His eyes flashed at her across the table, sending a thrilling shiver up and down her spine. "You've never been forced to calmly serve coffee every day to a woman like you."

With effort, Lucy stood and slid her sunglasses back on. "Yes, I think we should meet later," she said, trying to hold herself steady. "I've got something going with my tour group this afternoon, and then we can meet up for dinner."

Dev nodded and kept his gaze lowered respectfully. "I'll wait to hear from you."

Lucy turned and walked away, leaving the bill unsigned that one of the servers had dropped off at their table. She left Dev to handle that, because it was all she could do to walk away without letting him see how much he'd shaken her.

* * *

Following an afternoon spent at the Port Denarau Marina with a group of her guests, Lucy dropped her bags onto the bed in her bungalow with a deep sigh. She was still exhausted from the night before, and determined to never again indulge in karaoke on a group trip. The Mai Tais were just so *good*, and a person needed a certain amount of lubrication in order to get up on stage and sing Madonna songs, didn't she? Lucy flopped back onto the bed and kicked off her sandals. She needed a nap.

But there was still the matter of Dev. She closed her eyes to block out the afternoon light. Dev had shown up in *Fiji* to tell her...what? That he liked her? That he felt something for her? And now she needed to immediately call Nick and tell him that Dev was there, otherwise she would be back to square one with Nick following the awkwardness of her not immediately sharing with him that her ex-husband had popped up in her tour group in Morocco.

Lucy pushed herself into a sitting position, rustling the shopping bags next to her. She'd walked around the marina all afternoon with her newest travelers, stopping in at the Hard Rock Cafe at the marina for appetizers, and sitting in the sun while they watched the boats come and go. It had been an altogether pleasant afternoon—minus the hangover and the fact that Dev Lopez was waiting for her to get back to the resort.

She dug her phone from her purse and opened her text chain with Nick. The last thing he'd said to her was goodnight, which had been just a half hour earlier. Lucy quickly did the math: 4 p.m. in Fiji...midnight in Florida. That seemed reasonable. She hit the button to call him, but it went straight to voice mail. Strange. She tried again, voice mail again.

Lucy tapped out a quick text: *Hi, sorry I missed your goodnight! I was out with a group at the marina and I got you a few presents! I really really really need to talk to you—ASAP. It can't wait, so as SOON as you wake up, call me, okay? I don't care if it's midnight here! xo*

She hit send and waited, but it wouldn't deliver.

"Dammit," Lucy said absentmindedly, biting on the side of her thumb. She even tried turning off her phone and restarting it, but the message just hung there in limbo, not going anywhere.

In lieu of being able to talk to Nick, she decided to face the music and call Dev. He picked up on the second ring.

"Hello?"

"Hey," Lucy said, running a hand through her hair. "I'm back from the excursion. Where are you?"

"Laying on the deck of my bungalow. Wanna come over and go for a swim?"

"Uhhh," Lucy said, smiling against her will at the tone of his voice. It was hard not to fall back into their easy daily banter. "I'm not sure that's a great idea."

"Why? I've got towels, and I hear room service will deliver anything we want from any of the bars or restaurants."

"Dev," Lucy said, keeping her tone serious.

"Okay, I'm sorry. I honestly didn't mean for that to sound suggestive in any way. I was just trying to keep things low key."

"And you think us in bathing suits in a tiny swimming pool sipping wine and eating lobster is low key?"

"Not when you put it that way," he said, sounding chagrined. "I can be dressed in ten minutes. Can I see you? I'd really like the chance to start over. To talk better."

"You want to talk better?" Lucy laughed. "What does that even mean?" She pulled a t-shirt from one of her shopping bags and laid it flat across her thighs, running a hand over the colorful image of a black lab racing down the beach. She'd gotten it for Nick as a joke because the dog looked like Hemmie.

"It means I want to say the right things, Lucy. I want to look you in the eye and tell you what I really mean without pissing you off. Can you at least give me that chance?"

Lucy nodded, still touching the t-shirt.

"Are you nodding?" Dev asked. "Because I can't hear a nod."

"Yes," Lucy said, balling up the shirt and shoving it back into the bag. "I'm nodding. Yes."

"Great. So can we meet outside in ten minutes and go for a walk together?"

"I'll be out in ten." Lucy hung up before he had a chance to say anything else, and then she fell back flat onto the bed, rolling up like a potato bug with her face to the windows. The water beyond her deck was calm and smooth, lapping idly against the wooden bungalows like it didn't have a care in the world. Lucy wished she didn't have a care in the world, but she did, so she sat up and then stood, stretching her arms to the ceiling and sliding her feet back into her sandals.

She gave her appearance four minutes of sprucing: powder, blush, mascara, and a quick scrub with her toothbrush. Lucy ran a comb through her hair and twisted it up into a clip before digging a lipstick from her makeup bag and doing a quick swipe across her lips. That would have to work. She turned off the bathroom light and grabbed her purse on the way out.

The afternoon was beautiful and golden, and Dev was waiting on the wooden walkway with the light breeze blowing his t-shirt and causing it to ripple against his skin. He stood, hands on hips, as he watched Lucy close her door tightly.

"Hi," he said, sounding nervous but looking cool as a cucumber in his fitted black jeans and the ever-present black Doc Marten boots.

Lucy glanced at his outfit. "Is this your tropical vacation wear?"

"This isn't that different than Florida," Dev said, looking at the water and the palm trees that dotted the resort in the distance. "So I'm dressed the same way I dress at home."

"I was hoping you'd be in a Hawaiian shirt and some flip-flops," Lucy said, feeling far more anxious than she ever had in Dev's presence. "But this works too."

"Shall we walk a bit?" Dev took a few steps and Lucy followed suit, slipping her purse over one shoulder as they strolled down the wooden boards of the walkway.

They didn't say anything until they'd reached land, and as Lucy stepped gingerly onto the grass, she turned to Dev. "We could just go to the beach and sit by the water," she suggested. "Unless you feel like having a drink."

"I'm thinking a drink is in order." Dev blew out a breath that Lucy hadn't even realized he was holding. "If you don't mind."

"Sure. I'll just stick to sparkling water," Lucy said as they started to walk again. "Last night was a long one, and I paid for it all day."

They reached an outdoor bar that was situated on a manmade island of its own, accessible only by crossing over a small bridge and choosing an umbrellaed bistro table with a view of the water beyond. The bar itself had slats painted in an alternating rainbow of colors, and every umbrella was a different color. Tropical steel drum music played on the outdoor speakers.

After they were both seated and they'd ordered, Dev folded his hands on the table and took a long pause.

"So," he said, starting again. "First of all, I should say that on second thought, magically appearing here to accost you with my feelings was maybe not the wisest choice, so I apologize for that."

Lucy laughed. "Okay," she said, taking the tall glass of sparkling water that the waitress set in front of her and putting the straw between her lips. Dev immediately took a sip of his beer.

"However, I do still think that it holds a certain romantic appeal, and I'd like to make my case now that I'm here."

"Well," Lucy said, setting her drink down and looking out at the sunlight on the water. "Go ahead and tell me what you need to say."

Dev took a few deep breaths and Lucy snuck a look at him. It never stopped amazing her how mysterious and handsome he was. He looked and dressed like Lenny Kravitz hanging out at a record store on the weekend, and his general demeanor was one of wry amusement at the universe.

"Okay, here's the deal. The first time I saw you, when you walked into Beans & Sand, I thought, 'Wow, this girl is incredible.'"

Lucy flushed and reached for the straw in her drink. She swished the ice cubes around nervously.

"I mean, you're not only beautiful, but you're accomplished. Lucy, you're a doctor."

"Was—I was a doctor."

"Give yourself credit. You went through medial school. You're a brilliant woman. You had a serious career doing hard work, and you went through a lot before you picked yourself up off the floor and moved to a totally new place to start over. Alone. You don't know how much I admire that."

It was Lucy's turn to take deep breaths. "Thank you. That means a lot," she said quietly.

"And sure, I liked you. I was attracted to you, but I also knew you'd had some bad relationships—fairly recently—and I didn't want to get my hopes up only to be that guy you date while you're getting over your last break-up."

Lucy nodded. "So the concert? The one we went to back in February?"

"A date," Dev confirmed. "But I choked a little. I thought if you liked me, I'd get a signal of some sort, but you really seemed like you were just into the music."

"I liked you," Lucy said, her eyes drifting back to the water. "And I liked Nick, too, so don't get the idea that he was some sort of rebound or consolation prize. Neither of you felt like that to me. You're both really cool, really *different* men, and I enjoy the company of both of you."

"Which is a dilemma," Dev said, taking another sip of beer. It was his turn to squint at the water.

"Hell yeah it is," Lucy agreed. "Or at least it is now, because you're here and Nick is there, and you saying all these things is pretty confusing for me."

"I'm sorry for that, Lucy. You deserve better. I should have said something sooner, and I shouldn't have watched you fall for Nick without speaking up, but I did." He looked at her warily. "Do you want me to go home? If you want me to, I will."

Lucy squinted at him as the sun sank slightly and hit below their umbrella. "I don't want you to go home," she said, shaking her head. "All I want right now is to eat at the sushi bar and then go dancing."

Dev frowned; it clearly wasn't what he expected her to say.

"You want to...eat sushi? With me? And dance?"

"Yeah," Lucy said. She stood up. She took the last pull from her sparkling water and set the glass on the table. "There's a sushi restaurant inside the main building, and one of the bars has an outdoor dance floor with a live band under the stars. Will you take me?"

Dev drained his beer and stood up. He didn't even waste a second thinking about it. "I absolutely will."

Chapter 10

July 4

Fiji

Kona held the board steady in the water, trying to coax Mindy onto it after what felt like her eighty-sixth wipeout.

"You can do this," he said, his gaze boring into hers.

"No, I can't!" she shouted, swiping angrily at the water that dripped into her eyes. "You don't understand how many times I've fallen and gotten back up, and now I just can't."

Mindy could feel her own outrage and she knew it made her seem like a toddler, which annoyed her even more. But he didn't know how she felt, and she wasn't talking only about the number of times she'd been banged by the damn surfboard that day. Her conversation with Shayla about finding donors for her organization had been a turning point for Mindy, and had reminded her how fragile her happiness truly was. When it all came down to it, if her children weren't happy with her, then nothing was right with the world and she really needed to fix that. She couldn't keep putting everyone else's needs before her own.

"Come on," Kona said, turning toward the shore and tugging her surfboard along with him. "Let's go."

Mindy felt as if she were being scolded as she waded through the water after Kona's imposing figure, and she kept her eyes trained down, inwardly cursing herself for being such a baby.

On the sand, he lifted her board and carried it easily. "Follow me."

Mindy did as she was told, now wiping away hot tears along with the salty water, though Kona never once turned back to look at her, so she was pretty sure he had no idea that she was crying. Or maybe he did. He seemed like a man who understood how things were. Which was weird for Mindy, as both of her husbands had been men who distinctly *did not* understand how things were. Kevin had been a distant father, at best. And while she'd never wanted for anything, over time she'd found that pouring her heart and soul into motherhood while her husband casually watched from the sidelines, golf putter in hand as he waited for the chance to escape to the links, had driven a wedge between them. Followed by Arthur, who had never understood a single thing about Mindy except how to keep her happy in bed, and whose casual attitude about everything had nearly pushed her to the brink. Both had been her fault, in Mindy's mind; Kevin, because she'd been quick to hitch her wagon to the first socially appropriate, upwardly mobile boy who'd shown her any interest, and Arthur, because he'd been nothing but revenge on Kevin. After all, what woman in her right mind married her ex-husband's younger brother?

Mindy was busy mentally berating herself as she followed Kona farther down the beach, bypassing the surf shack altogether and taking a narrow path between two palm trees that led into thicker foliage. The part of her brain that had been hardwired to be alert to danger was pinging in her head somewhere—but just a faint echo—reminding her that she *should* be wary of a big, burly man leading her into a secluded area deep in the trees. But the rational part of her that ran on instinct reminded her that Kona had been nothing but a patient, gentle giant so far.

Finally, he stopped and turned to look at her. Mindy was

standing in a patch of sunlight that filtered through the treetops, making the droplets of water on her shoulders and chest glisten. Her breasts heaved slightly at the exertion of keeping up with Kona, even though he was the one carrying the surfboard and all she'd had to do was follow along, totally unencumbered.

"This is a place I'm not supposed to take you—can you keep a secret?"

Uh oh, Mindy thought, finally coming out of her own head enough to realize that she really had followed a man she barely knew into a "secret" area in what appeared to be a mini-jungle. She looked around, trying not to breathe too loudly and let on that her heart was racing like a thoroughbred horse let loose to run on a beach.

"Yes," she said, never taking her eyes off of him.

"This is my house," Kona said, setting her surfboard on the ground and resting it against a tree. "I built this."

Mindy frowned at the structure before her; she'd been so lost in thought that she hadn't even properly clocked the fact that there was a tiny bungalow tucked in amongst the trees. She looked at it now with awe: it was made of bamboo and covered with dried palm fronds, but rather than looking like some wonky playhouse made by children, it had the vibe of an artisanal craftsman. It was highly functional, but also beautiful.

"Wow," Mindy breathed, stepping forward on bare feet and realizing all at once that she was nearly naked as Kona watched her inspect his home. "You made this?"

"I did," Kona said. "It took me two years."

Mindy walked around the small dwelling, taking in the firmness of the structure and the quaint little wraparound porch he'd built. She admired the way he'd smoothed the wood and sanded everything until it shone.

"Can I?" she asked, stepping up to the doorway.

He nodded, his face a mask of anticipation and pride.

Mindy slid the latch off the front door and let it swing open. Inside the ceiling was peaked, and everything appeared handmade.

The table and chairs, the kitchen counter...the king-sized bed in one corner, with its white netting draped around it to keep mosquitos out.

"How do you have electricity?" she asked, still standing in the doorway as Kona waited outside for her. He made no move to come closer.

"My family owns this resort," he said simply. "My people have lived on this land for generations."

"So your family let you build this bungalow and live here?" She put one hand on the doorframe and turned back to him, realizing as she did that she either looked completely alluring there in her bikini and damp hair, or very much like an old, wet dog. But suddenly she didn't care, because the look in his eyes was not the look she saw in the eyes of the men she knew back home. Gone was the subtle appraising of value that she always picked up on. Absent was the calculation of her pros and cons as some man she was drinking martinis with stared at her across the table at a fundraiser, clearly wondering how their stock portfolios would line up, or whether their adult children might get along. Kona simply watched her with those clear, blue eyes, processing her without judgment.

"I lived for a while in Sydney," he said, leaning back against the trunk of a palm tree and folding his arms across his chest. "I worked in finance."

"What?" Mindy sputtered. She had not expected that. Not at all.

"I tried it, but it wasn't for me. Corporate work. Bland apartment with a gym and laundry service. Restaurant meals five or six nights a week. Women with no heart or soul."

Mindy blinked. "I can't even imagine you in that setting."

"That's because you've only seen me in this one."

"But you're so...calm. Self-possessed. Quiet. I can't imagine you in a boardroom, wearing a suit and tie."

"I'm sure there are photos somewhere if you need proof," he said with a smirk, arms still folded across his chest, back against the tree.

"What brought you back here?" Mindy watched as a light breeze blew all the foliage around. He'd truly chosen a beautiful spot to make his home, and in the distance, all she could hear was the rush of the ocean. This was paradise.

"Well, I like to think it was a change of heart," Kona said, smiling. "But one of my nephews referred to it as a 'massive meltdown of epic proportions,' and I can kind of see where he was coming from. I moved home, spent a few months surfing and sleeping in a tent, and then cut a deal with my family to be here on site year-round to keep an eye on everything. This," he said, gesturing at his bungalow, "is my payment for essentially being the resort manager. This life."

Mindy was still stunned. This man had barely spoken more than five words at a time since she'd met him, even as he'd coached her in the water, and she suddenly had his whole life story in the palm of her hand. And it was a fascinating one.

He looked up at the sky overhead. "But I'm happy. This is a dream life."

Mindy nodded. It did seem ideal. "I'm kind of flabbergasted. I really thought you were just a guy who ran a surf shack and gave lessons to tourists. But you're not."

Kona laughed and pushed himself away from the tree, finally taking a step toward her, which—for some reason—didn't make Mindy flinch at all. "No one is simply what they seem, Mindy. I would think you knew that at this point in your life."

She watched as he walked over to a small wooden box on his porch and opened the lid. Inside was a knife with a carved handle, which he picked up gently before walking over to a tree and reaching up to a hanging fruit. With a swift move, Kona cut the mango down and inspected it.

"You must be hungry," he said.

She realized then that he was right. She nodded.

As she watched, he held the knife expertly and sliced away the mango's outer skin the same way he might peel an apple. Each strip of the fruit's skin fell away, landing on the ground.

"Come here," Kona said, his manner the same as when he'd instructed her to follow him out of the ocean or into the trees.

Mindy stepped off his porch and walked over. On the blade of a knife, he held a juicy, slippery, perfect slice of citrus-colored mango. Lucy reached for it with her fingers, but he shook his head, watching her face.

Eyebrows raised, Lucy took a step closer. Kona held the knife above her, forcing her to tip her head back just slightly as they locked eyes. He lowered the dripping chunk of mango to her lips, watching as she opened her mouth and took it in with a laugh. Juice rain down her chin and she reached up to wipe it away, but Kona got it first, his big, rough hand catching it gently as she chewed the fruit.

"Oh my god," Mindy said, closing her eyes. "That's amazing."

"Right around my bungalow I have avocados, bananas, coconuts, and pineapple," he said, pointing with his knife at the trees that surrounded his home. "I wake up everyday and eat from my trees. More?" He sliced another piece of mango and held it out for her, but she nodded at him, indicating that he should eat next, so he did.

When they'd finished the fruit and Kona had tossed the mango husk and seed into the bushes, he bent over the wooden box on the porch again, pulling a rag from it to wipe his knife's blade. He put it all back in the box lovingly and shut it before standing up to look at Mindy again.

"I just wanted you to know that we all fall down sometimes," he said. "And there are days we don't want to get back on the surfboard, or it feels too hard or too tiring. But then we do. We remake ourselves every single day, Mindy, so the woman you've been in the past doesn't necessarily have anything to do with the woman you'll be in the future."

It was Mindy's turn to fold her arms across her body to cover her literal and metaphorical nakedness as they stood there in the trees. The sunlight had shifted so that it touched her entire body, drying her hair and leaving her exposed skin warm to the touch.

"Thank you," she said, meeting Kona's eyes. "For bringing me here. And for teaching me to surf."

He smiled at her but made no move to come closer. "You're

welcome. And now we should get you back because I have another lesson soon."

Mindy's heart dropped; she wasn't ready to leave his calm, reassuring presence, nor was she interested at the moment in saying goodbye to the first person who had truly surprised her in years. But once again she did as he asked, and she followed him back through the trees, down the narrow path, and out to the beach, where he deposited her at the surf shack with a final wave and a promise to see her in the morning for their next surfing lesson.

* * *

"Mom," Emory said, looking away from the phone screen as she FaceTimed with Mindy that afternoon. "The way you were with Shayla was uncool, uncool, uncool. Just no. A hundred times no."

"Excuse me?" Mindy put one hand up to the floppy hat that she wore, folding the brim so that it shaded her face. She was sitting poolside in a halter-necked one-piece that showed off her still quite ample assets. "Are you telling me how to be a mother?"

Emory sighed, sounding deeply disappointed. "No, but I am telling you how to be a *cool* mother. You need to help your daughter out, sis."

"Sis?" Mindy nearly laughed. "Since when am I your sis?"

"It's a term of endearment. But listen to me, because my time is on a budget, and that budget is running out." Emory leaned away from the screen for a moment, then popped back into view. "Sorry, I needed to sign off on something. I shouldn't tell you about it yet, but I'm in talks to develop my own beauty care line."

Mindy said nothing. She was well aware of her youngest child's desire to leave an impact on the world via her social media presence, and to be perfectly frank, Mindy wasn't that impressed.

"Anyhow," Emory went on. "I talked to Michael and we looped Shayla in, and we need to talk to you."

"I'll be home next week."

"No, they nominated me to be our mouthpiece, so here I go: Mom, you need to pull it together. Snubbing Shayla's charity work is just one small act of bad behavior in an even bigger tapestry of faux pas and missteps."

This time Mindy truly did laugh out loud. "Emory," she said, disbelieving her daughter's tone. "You're kidding me."

"Not at all. We've noticed that ever since your second *divorce*," she said, making a face like the word was a lemon in her mouth. "Ever since you dumped Uncle Arthur, you've been a wee bit out of pocket."

"I just—there's so much I want to address here," Mindy said, pulling off her oversize sunglasses and chewing on one end of them. "But I don't know where to start. How about with the phrase 'out of pocket'?"

"It means you're out of control," Emory said.

"Okay, then let's talk about your sister's charity, which—I might add—is not her doing charity work, it's actually *her job*."

"Which you disapprove of."

"I never said that," Mindy nearly shouted. "I said that I wasn't aware of the long-term reputation of the organization."

"Another way of snubbing, looking down on, turning up your nose," Emory said, ticking each item off on her fingers.

"Okay, we need to tap the breaks here," Mindy said, setting her sunglasses on the towel next to her thigh. "The three of you having powwows to talk about how crazy your old mom is kind of offends me."

Emory snorted. "Okay."

"I'm a grown woman, Em, and you need to show some respect for my choices. No, none of you approved of me marrying Arthur, and yes, I see now that it was a huge mistake, but honor my decisions. Let me be a person. The same goes for me not wanting to hand over the contact information for every human I know so that your sister's charity—"

"Her 'job,'" Emory said, making air quotes with her fingers.

"—fine, her job. Anyway, I don't need to sell everyone I know down the river to some organization that, for all I know, could be a total sham."

Emory sucked in a deep breath. "Ouch, Mother. You totally threw Shay under the bus with that comment."

Mindy was suddenly tired of her child's attitude and she held up a hand. "Okay, that's enough. I'll be home next week, and when I get home, I'll deal with all three of you. But for now, I'm on vacation in a gorgeous place, and I'm going to enjoy it. You three have fun with your side conversations about Crazy Mommy, and I'll have fun with—"

"A fifth of vodka and a younger man, would be my guess."

Mindy's went white and she lifted the brim of her hat, staring at Emory's haughty face on her phone screen.

Emory looked away. "I'm sorry," she said in a small voice. "I shouldn't have said that."

Mindy continued to stare and said nothing for a long minute. Finally, with as much patience as she could muster, she spoke. "I'll talk to you next week, Emory Jane. Goodbye." And then she ended the call.

But before she slipped her phone into her bag and laid back to soak up the sun, Mindy did one more thing: she sent a quick email to her financial adviser asking her to sell off a chunk of Emory's trust fund and to make a $500,000 donation to the Make-a-Wish Foundation. It was high time for her daughter to realize that the lifestyle she had was one of extreme privilege, and that not everyone her age had money to fall back on in the event that their career as a social media influencer went bust.

After she sent the message, she closed her eyes with a smile and tilted her face to the sun. She was starting to feel lighter already.

Chapter 11

July 4

Fiji

Heinrich tossed the hand towel he'd used for shaving over one shoulder, humming as he walked through his bungalow. Spencer had woken up after him and gone in to use the shower, so he took that little bit of quiet time to stand on the deck and stare out at the water, feeling like the king of his own castle for just a moment.

"Hey." Spencer reappeared at his side wearing only a towel. On her head.

"What the—Spencer!" Heinrich looked around to make sure that no one in the nearby bungalows could see her walking around in the altogether. "Are you crazy?"

She laughed wickedly and unwound the towel from her head. "Maybe."

"Come on," Heinrich said, feeling his eyes rove her lithe body. Was there anything more glorious than a woman's form? Heinrich wasn't sure that there was as he watched his decades-younger girl-friend spread the towel out on a chaise lounge and then stretch her body out, face to the sun.

"*You* come on, Heinz," she said petulantly, making a kissy face at him. She knew he hated to be called "Heinz," but from her, he'd take it. "I'm just going to let my hair dry here and get a little tan before we start working for the day."

Heinrich sighed and sank onto the chair next to hers. "We're never not working," he said with a sigh. "Speaking of, what do we have on Pietro? Did you get any shots of him looking out at the water, thinking about Avon?"

"Uh huh," Spencer said, putting her hands behind her head. It took every ounce of willpower that Heinrich had not to ravish her immediately, but he was hyper-aware of ever coming across as a desperate, randy old man (which he was quite certain that he probably was).

Heinrich looked out at the water and focused on a boat way off in the distance. Much too far in the distance for anyone on the vessel to get a close look at his girlfriend's breasts. Much too far away for any of the aggressively muscled, Nordic-looking deckhands that were undoubtedly on the boat to pull up and invite his girlfriend to come aboard for a day of luxury on the water, which would definitely be more appealing than another day of taking orders on the crew of a reality show.

"So," Heinrich said, trying to banish the Nordic deckhands that he'd completely invented out of his mind. "What else have you been up to? I feel like unless we're working on a shot together—"

"Or unless we're in bed and I'm working on *you*," Spencer said crassly.

"Yes," Heinrich agreed, "or that. But unless we're together, I have no idea what you're up to. Hopefully not hanging out at the beach topless."

Spencer opened her eyes and turned her head in his direction. She frowned at him, and it wasn't because the sun was in her eyes. "Are you jelly, Heinz?"

"Am I who? What? Oh," he said, catching onto the lingo just a hair too late. "Am I jealous. Well, maybe a little."

Spencer reached out her right hand and took his left one, lacing her fingers through his so that their hands dangled between the lounge chairs.

"Don't be, okay?" She gave him a searching look.

Heinrich cleared his throat; he wasn't accustomed to not having the upper hand, and it was even more foreign for him to be ceding any sort of romantic power to a woman half his age. And yet he found himself hanging on her every word, wondering if today would be the day she looked at him with his graying chest hair and deeply-etched crow's feet and realized that she could do so much better.

Spencer sat up and Heinrich's eyes immediately darted to the boat to make sure it was still far away.

"Listen," she said, still holding his hand and locking her eyes on his. "I sense that you feel like we're...somewhat imbalanced. Like I'm young and therefore I'm just here on a lark hanging out with you. And I'm not. I really like you. I don't waste my time with men who don't interest me, okay?"

Heinrich nodded, wanting desperately to look away from her hot gaze. He felt like a kid being scolded or put in his place, and it was too much. He wasn't used to this kind of emotional accountability or forthrightness from the women he dated.

"Okay, then I'll buck up," he said, offering her a smile. "I've never dated a woman twenty-five years younger than me, and there's a certain amount of insecurity that goes along with being the older party. It's hard to explain, but I catch myself looking around at other men and wondering if you might prefer their company. Like Todd, for instance. When you're talking to him it just looks so intense and I start to ask myself—"

"Well, stop asking yourself," Spencer interrupted. "Todd is just a guy. We're collaborating on something that I'll want to show you later, so don't even give him another thought. Or any other guy for that matter. I say who, I say how, I say when." She stared at him. "And Heinz, I say *you*."

Heinrich smiled at her and finally let his gaze drop to below her chin, which his eyes had been itching to do ever since she sat down.

"I say you look like a goddess," he said, reaching over and putting a hand on her flat stomach.

"Wanna go back inside?" Spencer winked at him.

"That'll make us late," he said, looking at his watch. "But you know what—to hell with it. Let's be late together."

* * *

Spencer had gotten through that day's shoot without any hiccups, and she was satisfied that she'd eased Heinrich's nerves. The poor man, walking around thinking he wasn't good enough to be with her because of their age difference when in actuality, he was just perfect in her eyes: old enough to know a bit about the world; smart enough to know how to act; accomplished in his field, and still sexy as hell.

But now that she was off-duty, she walked stealthily along the paths of the resort, thinking about the secret footage she had so far. She'd told Heinrich that she'd show him the project at some point and she truly meant that, but for the time being she felt it best to keep her furtive camerawork from him.

As Spencer reached the footbridge that crossed over the lazy river, she spotted Lucy, and she instinctively ducked into a secluded knot of shrubbery to watch and see what Lucy might do, and—more importantly—who she was with. Spencer turned on her camera and angled it in Lucy's direction.

The guy was over-the-top cool, in Spencer's opinion. He was taller than Lucy, dressed in loose linen pants and a white guayabera shirt with long sleeves that he'd rolled to the elbow and pushed up to reveal his smooth brown skin. He wore flip-flops and a pair of sunglasses that made him look like a rockstar. He and Lucy stopped to look at the lazy river together, and as they did, he lightly placed a hand on her lower back.

Interesting—had Lucy met someone at the resort? Spencer hadn't seen this guy yet, and from the way he moved, she knew she would have picked him out of a crowd immediately if he'd been roaming the grounds of the Frangipani Fiji resort.

Spencer zoomed in on the pair as they turned their heads to look at one another, talking and laughing animatedly. This was good. A budding romance right under Spencer's nose that she could integrate into her footage. Now all she needed was to get closer, to talk to Lucy more and find out how she'd met this dude. That—added to what she was getting of Mindy Shultz and the hot guy whose surfboard Mindy was trying to wax—could actually add up to a little mini storyline for Spencer to work on and present to the network. This side project could make a name for her in a way that being an assistant on the set of a reality show never would. She crouched down behind the bushes and kept her lens focused on Lucy and her island lover, hoping to catch something scintillating. A kiss, maybe—or perhaps a quick amorous moment there in the grass. Nothing unseemly, of course, but Spencer had an eye for what would catch her viewers' attention, and this little union of two beautiful people at a tropical resort was just the ticket.

Chapter 12

July 4

Fiji

Lucy laughed, putting her hands to her chest.

"Stop!" she pleaded with Dev as she bent over at the waist, trying to catch her breath.

They'd stayed out late the night before, sharing a sushi platter and then dancing until well after midnight at the bar with a roof that opened up to reveal a million stars. The live band had played everything from Big Band music to 80s hits, and Lucy had laughed and let loose like she hadn't in years, surprised at the way Dev moved on the dance floor. He was so reserved sometimes that she hadn't expected him to pull her close, their bodies sweaty from exertion, their cheeks aflame with excitement. There they were, thousands of miles from everyone they knew, acting like a couple of kids let loose on a playground.

But Lucy had stopped it there, saying goodnight firmly on the boardwalk that led to their bungalows, and Dev had accepted her limit without even a flicker of an indication that he'd expected more.

When she woke up that morning, Lucy had felt exhilarated, helped no doubt by the fact that she'd stuck to sparkling water all night, and she'd bounded out of bed to see if Dev was ready for breakfast. After all, he was just a friend visiting from home. At least to her. She'd listened to what he'd had to say, processed his reasoning for flying to Fiji, and decided that while it was a grand gesture, the best she could do was to have a good time with him without crossing any boundaries. As for Nick, well, she'd tried to reach him several more times, and while his phone was now ringing and her messages were delivering, she was getting no response.

But she'd brushed that aside for the time being, famished as she was from a night of dancing, and met up with Dev for a huge brunch of pancakes and sausages before they headed out to explore the entire resort from one end to the other.

"Stop!" she shouted again, laughing now as he described the way that Howard, the man Honey was currently dating back home, had pinched Honey's bottom before they slid into a booth at the coffee shop for their first date. "They had their first date at Beans & Sand? That's so cute!" she wailed, imagining Honey being moved on by a guy old enough to remember the Dust Bowl.

"They did," Dev said, nodding as he put his hand on Lucy's lower back to guide her on. "And old Howard not only gave her booty a little pinch, but he also told her she looked like Ava Gardner."

"I can't even with this story," Lucy laughed. "Howard's got so many slick moves."

"Seriously though," Dev agreed. "I took notes."

"Keep your hands off my butt," Lucy said, holding up a finger in a jokey warning.

"I'm not old enough to pull that off yet." Dev said. "But I figure in about fifty years I might be able to try it and not get slapped."

"Maybe." Lucy considered it. "But times have changed."

"For the better?"

"In some ways. I think women still put up with far more than they should, and weirdly, I think that by embracing our sexual freedom in the way that we have over the past decade or two, we've given up a little of our mystery. But I'm kind of old-fashioned that way, so don't go by my opinion."

"Hey, don't discount where you stand on something. Your points are as valid as the next person's," Dev said. He stopped walking and looked at her seriously. "And I don't disagree. I tend to prefer some mystery. There's nothing in this 'swipe left, swipe right' culture for me. You can call me old-fashioned too, but I still like going on a date where I don't know how the night is going to end."

Lucy smiled at him. "You're an interesting character."

"Aren't we all?"

They strolled on, making their way to the front desk so that Lucy could double-check their plans for the Bula Festival over the next two days. As the glass doors to the lobby slid open to let them in, Lucy leaned closer to Dev and whispered. "I like your new outfit, by the way."

He put his hand on her back again—just gently, but enough to be gentlemanly in a way that Lucy never failed to notice—and smiled down at her. "Hey, you called my island fashion into question, so I had to remedy that with a quick trip to the resort shops."

Lucy reached out and ran a hand down the button flap of his shirt, realizing as she did that it was an extremely familiar move to make with a man whose presence in Fiji had not at first been a welcome one. She looked up at him, surprised at her own forwardness.

"Lucy?"

A voice echoed through the lobby and she stopped in her tracks. Dev stopped with her, a hand still on her back. She could feel the blood drain from her face.

"Lucy, what the hell is going on?" It was Nick, standing at the front counter with a suitcase at his feet and his wallet in one hand, a credit card pulled out to hand over to the woman behind the desk.

"Nick," Lucy said breathlessly, pulling away from Dev and crossing the lobby like she was on fire. "Nick, oh my god. I've been calling you and texting. Where have you been? What are you doing here?"

She looked around wildly, realizing as she did that there were people sitting on couches beneath the potted palms, watching with mild curiosity. (There was also, though Lucy didn't notice, Spencer with her camera in hand, standing in one corner of the lobby discreetly after having followed Lucy and Dev in through the sliding doors.)

"I wanted to surprise you," he said, laying his credit card on the counter without looking at the woman who was about to swipe it. "I missed you."

Lucy stood there, a foot of distance between them, her eyes on his face. She could feel her skin go hot with shame; she'd been having such a good time talking to Dev and just hanging out that she'd forgotten for a moment how it would all look to someone on the outside. Particularly how it might look if it got back to Nick, though she'd never once considered for a moment that he might show up and observe it with his own eyes. God, she was so dumb.

"Nick," she said softly, closing the distance between them and throwing her arms around him. As she did, she realized that the woman at the front desk was about to run his card. "No," she said, letting go of Nick and looking at him. "Don't get a room. Come on, you're staying with me." She took both of his hands in hers and then looked at the girl holding Nick's card. "Please don't run that."

"I'm sorry, ma'am," the young woman said, smiling politely. "Mr. Epperson has reserved a bungalow, and I'm afraid we'll have to charge him for at least one night's stay, whether he uses the room or not."

Just then, Jasmine, the beautiful woman who'd been manning the desk the day that Mindy had tumbled into the lobby with her dogs and her piles of Louis Vuitton luggage, swept into the conversation, lowering her voice discreetly.

"I'll handle this, Josephine," she said, setting an elegant hand on the younger woman's forearm and dismissing her gently. "We're so glad you're here," she said to Nick. "I trust your flight was easy?"

Nick relaxed a little, letting himself be wooed by a woman whose manner was, by nature, soothing and attentive. "Not really. I got stuck in New Zealand for twelve hours, and I haven't slept in about a day and a half." He laughed tiredly. "But I'm here now, so..." He looked back at Lucy briefly. "I guess I'll pay for the night on my own, and then stay with her for the rest of the trip."

"Paying for a night won't be necessary, Mr. Epperson," Jasmine said, tapping at the computer keys as she scanned the screen. "We'll just send your bags to Ms. Landish's room and you can go ahead and get some rest."

"Thank you," Lucy said, leaning toward the desk without letting go of either of Nick's hands. "I really appreciate you being so accommodating."

"No problem at all," Jasmine said with a smile, handing back Nick's credit card along with an extra key to Lucy's bungalow. "Enjoy your stay."

As Lucy and Nick turned away from the counter, she remembered with a start that Dev was still standing there, watching. Seeing his face and feeling Nick tense up at her side was like having a bucket of icy water dumped over her head.

Nick cleared his throat and said nothing. Out of solidarity, Lucy slipped her hand back into his and glanced around the lobby. The few people scattered about appeared to have gone back to looking at their phones or whatever else they'd been doing, and Spencer had taken a seat in a chair on the far side of the giant open area, where she was casually looking at her camera in her lap and not garnering any attention whatsoever.

"So," Dev said, putting both hands into the pockets of his newly purchased linen pants. He rocked back on his heels and waited for Nick to speak.

"What are you doing, dude?" Nick finally asked, running his free hand through his hair. With his other hand, he was still holding Lucy's, though his grip had tightened and she winced. "Why did you come here?"

"I felt like a vacation," Dev said, keeping his face neutral. Lucy gave him credit for that in the moment, as the slightly antagonistic vibe between Nick and Dev at home sometimes caused him to smirk. "You made your trip to St. Barts seem like such a good time that I figured I'd give it a shot."

Nick breathed in and then let it out. "You thought you'd fly to Fiji on a whim? To where my girlfriend is?"

"Nick," Dev said, pulling his hands from his pockets and holding them up in surrender. "Dude, I came here of my own volition—none of this was Lucy's idea, and I'll be honest, she wasn't completely thrilled to see me."

It was on the tip of Lucy's tongue to interject something reassuring here, but her brain told her to hold back, so she did, squeezing Nick's hand instead.

"Well, when you two walked in a minute ago she was looking pretty happy."

Dev let his hands fall. "I don't know what to say to that, man. We were just talking and laughing. Nothing has happened."

"We went dancing," Lucy blurted, regretting it instantly. She'd been holding the fact that Dev was there in Fiji like a bird in her hand, waiting to release it the minute she got Nick on the phone, but now that he was here next to her and she no longer had that piece of information to give him, she felt like she needed to say something honest, something that would make him see that she wasn't hiding anything.

He turned to look at her incredulously. "What?"

"Last night," Lucy rushed on. "We had dinner and then we went dancing, but nothing happened, Nick. I promise you. It's not like that —at least not for me."

Nick nodded slowly, his head bobbing as he thought about that. "I might just be tired from traveling, but this is all sounding really sketchy for me, Lucy. I'm not accusing you of sleeping with Dev," he said, pausing as a gasp rang out from the couch just feet away from them. An older woman with a magazine in her lap was listening, mouth agape like she was watching a drama unfold before her very eyes. Which she kind of was.

"God, Nick," Lucy said in a whispered hiss. "Give me a break. I would never."

"Ouch," Dev said, pulling a wounded face. "I mean 'never' is kind of harsh."

Lucy turned and gave him a sharp look. "Not the time for jokes."

Nick took a step back from them as one of the bellhops came and picked up his suitcase, setting it on a rolling cart to wheel away and deliver to Lucy's bungalow.

"I'm gonna take a nap," he said, shaking his head. "If you just point me in the right direction, I'll find my own way."

"No, Nick. I'm coming. I'll come with you." Lucy turned her back on Dev and walked toward her boyfriend, ready to placate him as much as necessary to start re-building whatever trust had been broken by the situation at hand.

"No, seriously. I just need a nap and then I'll talk to you later. Which way do I go?"

Jasmine handed a printed map of the resort across the counter helpfully, circling the wooden walkway that led to Lucy's bungalow and then putting a star over the one that was hers. "Here you go," she said, stepping away from the counter tactfully and disappearing so that she wasn't in the way.

"I'll text you when I wake up," Nick said. He walked straight ahead and through the sliding doors, disappearing into the sunlight.

"Well," Lucy said, blowing out the breath that had been trapped in her chest.

"Well," Dev agreed, setting his hands on his hips as he blew out an exaggerated breath of his own.

They stood there and gave each other one long, last look, then parted ways without another word.

Chapter 13

July 4

Fiji

The heat of the afternoon was getting to Mindy, as was the call she'd had with Emory that morning. She'd gone to the spa and tipped 300% for both her facial and her massage, and when she came of the spa with a whole new mental state, she had to admit that she did feel better.

Lucy had let everyone in the group know that plans for the Bula Festival were on for that evening, and that the resort was providing transport from the lobby where they could take part in the carnival atmosphere and all the fun. From what Jasmine had explained to Mindy at the front desk on her way into the spa, the Bula Festival was an annual event that celebrated Fiji's culture and its people. There would be fire-walking, dancing in traditional island clothing, beauty pageants, food, games, music, and parade floats, and it would be going on for the next week. It was perfect timing for all of the island's American guests that the first day of the festival happened to be on July 4th, that way anyone who was feeling a tad bit homesick for any of the usual Independence Day activities could track down a hot dog or some local fare, and sit down to watch people twirling fire as the sun went down.

After her trip to the spa, Mindy had changed into navy blue silk shorts and a red tank top with a pair of white Converse in honor of the 4th of July, then signed up for the shuttle to the festival. She'd told Dean he could skip the afternoon walk with Bridger and Bagley and instead she'd leashed them up and taken them directly toward the part of the resort where Kona's beach shack and his hand-crafted bungalow were located. When she'd mentioned to him during their surf lesson that her dogs were on the island with her, he'd told her that he'd love to see them, so she figured that afternoon was as good a time as any.

Mindy rounded the bend of the sandy path, holding firm to the dogs' leashes as they dragged her on, eager to get to the source of the rushing sound of water. As soon as they crested the sand and saw the waves, the dogs started to bark with excitement.

"You want to go in the water?" Mindy asked, calming them so that she could unhook their collars and let them run free. "Be good, okay?" she yelled fruitlessly, watching as they bounded across the sand, racing for the ocean.

"Are these the infamous beasts?"

Mindy turned her head in surprise; Kona had materialized over her shoulder.

"Yes," she said, smiling. "You said you wanted to see them and they needed an afternoon walk, so I thought I'd bring them to the beach for a good, hard run. I hope I'm not coming at a bad time. Do you have a surf lesson starting soon? Or customers in the shop? I can round them up and make sure I'm not in your way at all—"

"Mindy," Kona said, laughing. "You're not in my way."

Mindy breathed a sigh of relief. "Good."

"Do you ever pause though? I've never known a woman who can race from one thought to the next without a moment of downtime like you can."

It was Mindy's turn to laugh. "Have you known many women? Because that's what it's like inside our heads *all the time.*"

"Wow." He was wearing a white t-shirt and a pair of clean khaki cargo shorts. Bare feet, of course, but his hair was damp and combed back from his face. "It's like you're doing mental gymnastics all the time. No wonder women live longer than men."

She looked out at the water and watched as Bridger and Bagley jumped over the waves, biting at the foamy water and tumbling over one another like much smaller puppies.

"You're gonna want to hose those two down before you let them back into the bungalow. There's an outdoor hose behind the main building that's always hooked up, so if you take them back there and just turn it on, you can wash them off."

"Thank you. Good thinking." They stood there quietly for a moment, watching the dogs play. "Hey, I'm going to the Bula Festival tonight," Mindy said, casting a glance in his direction. Butterfly wings beat in her chest and she felt like a girl asking a boy to a school dance or something. "Would you want to come with me?"

Kona was still. He kept his eyes trained on the water for what felt like ages and Mindy wished she could reel her words back in and not have asked the man whose family owned the resort if he wanted to take a chartered bus with her to an event that he'd probably been to a million times. She felt like an idiot.

He finally turned to look at her. "How about if *you* come with *me?*" Kona asked.

Relief washed over Mindy and she grinned at him. "Yeah? You want me to come with you?"

"I'll meet you at the front entrance to the lobby at seven o'clock, if that works for you. My car is parked in the lot and we can drive that."

Mindy giggled. "So then you don't want to ride the charter bus?"

Kona folded his arms and Mindy tried not to watch as the muscles and tendons flexed under his smooth skin. "I've got a Jeep. Let's take that."

"Deal," Mindy said, feeling like someone had shaken up a can of soda in her stomach and then popped the top. "I'd better take these dogs back and get them washed up. Boys!" she called, walking closer to the water and cupping her hands around her mouth. "Bridge! Bags! Come on!"

The dogs stopped what they were doing and glanced back at her, panting. They looked like two little boys who'd just been told that it was time to come in and clean up before dinner.

"Here, let me," Kona said, walking into the water. The waves washed over his calves as he put two fingers in his mouth and let out a loud, piercing whistle. As if on cue, the dogs turned again and then raced for the shore, stopping short at Mindy's feet.

"How did you do that?" she asked with wonder. "Sometimes I think they purposely don't listen to me—just like children!"

"Eh, sometimes you just have to treat them like children and make them listen."

Mindy smiled. He had such a way about him, such a calm, peaceful demeanor that was at the same time commanding and confident. It was a huge turn-on for her.

"See you at seven?" Kona asked, walking backwards toward the shore as he watched Mindy bend over to re-clip the dogs' leashes.

She looked up at him. "It's a date," she said, immediately wondering whether it really was a date.

But rather than confirm or clarify, Kona simply smiled before turning and heading back to his surf shack.

Kona's jeep was in fact a drop-top that he drove at high speeds around the windy roads, causing Mindy to squeal with abandon and hold tight to the dashboard. It had been years since she'd ridden with a guy who drove like a sixteen-year-old who'd filched the keys to his parents' car, and there was something freeing about the way the wind whipped through her hair and carried her screams of laughter away as they dipped and dove around every bend.

"You're crazy!" Mindy shouted, turning to look at him with absolute glee on her face.

"I know these roads like the back of my hand!" Kona yelled back, holding the steering wheel confidently with one hand as his hair blew around in the twilight.

Mindy reached over and put her hand on top of his as it rested on the stick shift. As she did, he glanced her way and then back at the road.

Once they'd parked on a side street and put the Jeep's top up, Kona offered Mindy his arm. It was such a charming, gallant move that it caught her by surprise, but it certainly didn't stop her from smiling and slipping her hand through the crook of his strong arm. They strolled through town that way, swept along with the rest of the people making their way to the heart of the festivities.

Darkness had officially fallen, and even from a few blocks away, the sounds and lights of the carnival atmosphere punctured the night. People were laughing and screaming from atop the rides, food was grilling in outdoor pits, and the bright neon lights of different attractions lit up the sky.

"It's not just fun and games," Kona said, pulling her closer to his side as they let a large group dressed in matching printed shirts pass them by. "The Bula Festival is all about Fijian culture. Sure, there's fun to be had, but you can also see some of the things we take pride in."

Mindy watched his face in profile as he spoke. She was having the kind of out of body experience people sometimes have as she listened and wondered exactly how she'd been transported from her life in Manhattan to an exotic island in the South Pacific. How was she possibly walking arm-in-arm with a totally zen—and totally gorgeous—man who spent his life next to the ocean, talking and laughing as if they'd known each other for years? It seemed surreal.

"Take the firewalkers, for instance," Kona was saying, leading her over to where a group of people had gathered. "It is considered a gift from the spirit gods to be able to walk on fire without injury. Traditionally, men of the Sawau tribe abstained from sex and from eating coconuts for two weeks before a fire walk, and they always came through it unharmed."

"There are men who can abstain from sex for two weeks?" Mindy joked.

Kona gave her a wry smile and pulled her closer to where people were gathered around a bed of red-hot coals. "See?" He pointed at two men in traditional grass skirts. Their brown chests were bare, and on their head they wore wreathes of greenery. They stood huddled, heads together as they talked seriously. "They will each take a turn, and when they're done, you'll see: they'll be unscathed."

Mindy's eyes were fixed on the glowing coals. "I've never seen this in person. In fact, I always wondered if it was somehow a trick—like a magic trick."

"Definitely not. And these guys are actually doing it to raise money for charity."

"Which charity?" Mindy's head snapped toward him. "I love charities."

Kona raised a hand at a woman in a grass skirt with a floral wreath on her head. She walked over with a smile. "Brochure?" she offered. He smiled at her and took one.

"Here you go," Kona said, opening the flyer. "They're going to brave the fire walk to raise money for a charity that supports education for Pacific and Caribbean women and girls. You can check any of the following boxes," he read, "or write in a donation amount of your choice."

Mindy listened thoughtfully. "Education for women and girls. I like it." She held out her hand and he passed her the flyer. "Let me get my pen." Mindy dug through her purse and pulled out a ballpoint pen. "Can I use your back?"

Kona turned around and let her put the flyer against his firm back so that she could write. She skipped over all the boxes: ten, twenty, fifty, a hundred dollars—not enough. On the write-in line, Mindy scrawled $20,000 and then included her email, phone number, and mailing address for them to send a bill. Without showing Kona, she folded the flyer in half and gestured for the girl in the grass skirt to come back over with the box in which she was collecting donations. She slipped it through the slot and put her pen back into her purse.

"That's good of you to make a donation," Kona said, smiling at her. "Are you always this generous?"

Mindy smiled. He undoubtedly assumed she'd given twenty or fifty dollars, which was fine with her. "I've been fortunate in my life, and I like to support organizations that do good things," she said, turning to focus on the men as they prepared to walk across the coals.

The sun was long gone, and aside from the bright orange of the fire on the ground, the only light was from tiki torches that burned all around the area. Mindy took a step closer to Kona, hoping he might not notice.

"Thank you all for coming," a man with an extremely large stomach that hung over his own grass skirt bellowed to the crowd. "We will have silence now for Joe and Moses as they prepare for their walks. If you have not yet had a chance to make a donation to our wonderful charity, please consider doing so." He put his palms together in front of his chest and took a deep breath. "Okay, here we go!"

The crowd sucked in a collective breath and seemed to hold it as the first man approached the scalding coals with a look of determination. Mindy slipped her hand into Kona's and held it, unable to tear her eyes away as the shirtless man took one final inhale and stepped forward, putting his bare feet in the fire. A small gasp went through the onlookers, but it was clear from the deep concentration etched on the face of the firewalker that he heard nothing. He just kept going— one foot, then the other, then the other—as a look of complete and utter calm washed over him.

Within seconds, he'd done it. He'd walked the length of the hot coals and stepped back onto the cool sand, bending forward at the waist and then standing straight again with a fist pumped in the air. A loud cheer roared through the crowd and Mindy joined in, shouting for him as she looked up at Kona.

"That was amazing," she said, still holding his hand.

"That was complete belief in oneself," Kona replied. "You can have no doubts, no second thoughts about your own capabilities."

Mindy shook her head. "I'm not sure I could do it."

"Sure you could." Kona frowned at her, tilting his head as if admiring a strange and foreign creature. "Why could you not?"

Mindy was silent for a moment as she watched the second man queue up and stare down the hot coals. "I don't think I have that kind of belief in myself."

Without hesitation, Kona spoke. "Sure you do. You get up every single day and walk through fires of your own. We all do."

Mindy blinked a few times. It was so simple when he put it that way. Of course they all walked through fires of their own, each and every day. That's what life was: fire walk after fire walk, with deep breaths and the confidence to always keep putting one foot in front of the other.

"You're so right," she said. "My god, I never thought of it that way."

The second man took his first steps and everyone watched in awe as he cleared the coals just like the first walker. A round of applause and another cheer followed his finish, and then Kona leaned close to Mindy's ear.

"Want to get some lovo with me?" he asked.

"Sure," she said without hesitation, though she had no idea what she was agreeing to. "What is it?"

"Lovo is a traditional Fijian dish." Kona led her through the crowd and past a band playing music as more people in traditional dress did a choreographed dance. Mindy's eyes stayed on the dancers, even as they passed by them. "First you dig a hole in the ground and fill it with stones which are heated by fire. Then you place the food in, which is usually fish or chicken wrapped in banana leaves. You cover it all and let it cook for hours, and when you take it out, the food is delicious. You'll love it."

"But will I *lovo* it?" Mindy couldn't resist the easy Dad Joke. She giggled at her own stupid wit.

Kono laughed appreciatively. "That's cute. And yes, you will."

The music and the laughter followed them as they walked, and Mindy realized that she hadn't been that happy and carefree in as long as she could remember. In that moment, she would have followed Kona anywhere.

Chapter 14

July 4

Fiji

The Bula Festival was turning out to be a lot less fun for Lucy than it was for Mindy. First of all, both Nick and Dev had insisted on coming, and now that they were there, neither was willing to leave her side. It seemed as though the nap had infused Nick with a new sense of purpose, which appeared to essentially be to glue himself to Lucy's side. And Dev, while contrite that afternoon in the lobby when Nick had arrived, seemed to have redoubled his efforts to show Lucy that he'd made a mistake by not coming on strongly enough back on Amelia Island.

They'd ridden over on the chartered bus with a load of other resort guests and the majority of the Holiday Adventure Club group, and though Lucy knew it wasn't her job to count heads like a teacher leading a field trip or anything, she still felt responsible for the safety and happiness of her travelers. To that end, she was trying her best to keep a smile plastered on her face as the three of them wandered through the festival, stopping to watch a beauty pageant filled with women wearing sashes across their chests and as single hibiscus flower tucked behind their right ears. They all wore identical dresses of a purple satin material, and while Lucy, Nick, and Dev watched, each woman took a turn walking in front of the crowd, smiling and waving as she passed the onlookers. Family and friends cheered for the young ladies, and Lucy applauded along with them, trying to stall and stay away from any situation that would involve the three of them having to be somewhere that would require them to fill the silence with conversation.

Eventually Nick led them on, and as they reached the carnival area, he took Lucy's hand. "Let's go on the ferris wheel," he said, not waiting for her to reply.

"Nick," she protested, exhausted already from the feeling that no matter what she did or said, it wouldn't be the right thing. "I'm not sure I'm up for that." But he'd already taken out his wallet and paid, so Lucy clamped her mouth shut and stepped up to the line behind him. Much to her chagrin, Dev paid for a solo ticket and got into line right behind them.

"This is a seat for two, buddy," Nick said, giving Dev an insincere smile.

"That's fine," Dev said, returning the faux grin. "I'm not afraid to be alone."

It was on the tip of Lucy's tongue to scream at both of them for acting like a couple of teenage boys who were fighting over the same girl, but she realized that this was neither the time nor the place. In addition, they were grown men—business owners with their wits about them—and she really needed to let them come to their senses and realize that they were acting ridiculous.

On the ferris wheel, Lucy sat as far away from Nick as she could, hoping her annoyance was palpable. The ride operator moved the wheel and then paused again so that Dev could get on the seat behind them, which irked Lucy even more. Once the seats were filled, the wheel turned smoothly, lifting Lucy and Nick up until they crested the peak of the wheel and began to fall again. She stayed quiet.

"I understand that you're feeling pressed here," Nick said,

leaning his elbows on the bar that ran across their laps. "But you have to imagine how I'm feeling."

Lucy finally broke her silence, turning to him with a look of disbelief. "You could have at least told me you were coming, which would have given me the chance to tell you that Dev was here," she hissed, glancing behind them to see if Dev was close enough to hear them. She figured over the noise of the band playing and the people shouting below, he probably couldn't. "As it was, you showed up like a jealous boyfriend looking to catch me doing something wrong."

"It wasn't like that, Lucy," Nick said, elbows still on the bar, fingers splayed as he explained. "I just found out that Dev had come here and I freaked out. I knew he always had some kind of feelings for you, but I couldn't believe he'd act on them and come down here knowing that you and I are together. And when you two walked in..." He shook his head and looked out at the crowds below. "I mean, come on."

"No, *you* come on. I've known Dev as long as I've known you. I was pissed when he showed up but I made my peace with it and we went out like friends. We danced, we had a good time, and that was it. Don't you trust me?"

Nick took a long beat before answering. "Lucy," he said, turning his head to her as they passed over the ground again, then started the rotation back up to the top. "I trust you. But life is hard and sometimes things aren't fair. It would be unfair to have Dev fly down here and steal the girl I like while I sit at home moping. It would be unfair to trust you and then have you come back and tell me that you'd fallen for him down here. Life is just so..."

"Unfair?" Lucy asked, her eyes on his. She'd softened a bit listening to him, and she knew that included in his list of things that were unfair was losing his daughter, Daisy, to cancer as a toddler. Nick was well-versed in the unfairness of life, and so far he hadn't shown himself to be an alarmist at all. He was a calm, deeply pragmatic man, and she knew that if he felt that things were going to shake out unfairly, he'd only have wanted to level the playing field by showing up and making sure he was still in the game.

Lucy was about to scoot closer to him and link her arm through his when they once again reached the bottom, only this time the ride stopped and the young kid running it stepped up and unlatched their bar. "There you go," he said, waiting for them to get off and step out of the way.

In seconds, Dev was off the ride and standing behind them. "Where to next?" he asked, hands on hips. "Should we watch the parade?"

Just then, the grand marshal of the parade appeared at the end of the paved street beyond the carnival area. He was riding on the back of a horse, followed by what looked to be a high school band that hadn't yet been instructed to kick off the music.

"We could always get something to eat," Nick suggested. "I saw a whole line of food carts and stands over there while we were at the top of the ferris wheel." He pointed east.

"How about you grab us some snacks, and Lucy and I will save us a parade spot," Dev suggested.

Lucy felt like a ping-pong ball being volleyed back and forth between them, and with each thing they said, the anger boiled yet another degree hotter within her.

Nick's nostrils flared. He took a step toward Dev just as the band struck the first notes and started their slow march behind the grand marshal and his horse. Everyone around them turned their attention toward the parade, but Nick and Dev were suddenly locked in a verbal battle right then and there. No more of their passive-aggressive Mr. Nice Guy routines.

"How about you grab the next flight back to Miami?" Nick offered, taking another step into Dev's personal space.

The band grew closer and got louder, and on its heels came the first parade float, draped in a rainbow of flowers and holding several men dressed in rugby uniforms. Lucy tried to ignore the parade and instead she turned her attention back to Nick and Dev.

"I'm not going home yet," Dev said, not backing away from Nick, though Nick was slightly taller. "As far as I can tell, you and Lucy aren't married. And until she tells me that I have zero chance in hell of her ever dating me, I'm going to assume that she might."

Lucy scratched her head, trying to find the words that needed to be said. None came to her.

"Oh?" Nick looked around, incredulous. "Lucy hasn't told you no? You've been here for more than twenty-four hours, and she hasn't told you in no uncertain terms that she's off the market?" He turned to her, waiting. "Lucy?"

Again, she had nothing, her mouth hanging open slightly, eyes wide as she looked first at Nick, then at Dev and back at Nick again.

"Seriously?" Nick was aghast. He shook his head and took a step back. "Okay...I just...I don't know what to say here."

"Nick," Lucy said, finally finding her words. She reached out for him but he took another step back. "It's not at all the way you're making it out to be."

"Did Dev show up here out of the blue?"

"Yes," Lucy said.

"Did you express some shock at his arrival, followed quickly by a recovery that found you dancing with him all evening and *not* saying explicitly that you have a boyfriend and are unavailable?"

"I mean—"

"Gotcha." Nick's eyes fell to the ground. He looked hurt. Disappointed. A little angry. When he looked back up, it was at Lucy and not Dev. "Here's what I think we should do."

Another float passed by, this one holding a beauty queen on a throne, her crown twinkling under the street and carnival lights as she waved at first one side of the street, then the other. Behind her was a band of older men, with one wailing on the saxophone as they trailed her float.

"I think," Nick said, "that you should consider yourself single for the rest of the time we're here. You can go out with Dev, or you can go out with me, but not at the same time." He gestured at the little triangle they were making there at the Bula Festival. "Not like this."

"But Nick—"

"No," Nick interrupted her. "This is clearly not one hundred percent settled for you, and it needs to be. It absolutely needs to be. You can either spend time laying next to me in bed while I read little snippets out loud to you from Malcolm Gladwell or Dostoyevsky, or you can—" (here, he gestured wildly with one hand) "hop on the back of his motorcycle and hit outdoor concerts until your heart's content. But you can't have both."

Lucy swallowed hard at the mention of climbing on the back of Dev's motorcycle. It was still her hope that Nick had no idea about that night she'd ridden out to the beach with him. As she searched her boyfriend's face, she realized how royally she was screwing things up. Here was a man who would fly to Buffalo for her to help deal with her family. Here was someone who would walk the beach with his dog in her absence, missing her. Here was the kind of boyfriend who got up early to make her coffee and bring it to her in bed. Lucy wanted to fling herself in front of the next parade float for even hurting Nick a tiny bit; he deserved so much better.

"So okay," Nick said, looking wounded beyond words. "I'm gonna head back to the resort and you and Dev can have this evening. Can we have breakfast tomorrow?"

Lucy felt a dangerous bile climbing her esophagus; this wasn't what she wanted at all. But Nick was already retreating.

"Nick," she said, reaching out a hand but not moving in his direction.

"I'll sleep on the foldout couch in the bungalow," he said. "See you whenever you get in." And with that, he turned and walked away.

Wisely, Dev said nothing, but Lucy still spun and stared at him angrily anyway. "Was this what you wanted?"

Dev's eyes burned into hers. He looked—not sad, not apologetic exactly, and certainly not contrite—if anything, he seemed excited by

104

the upheaval. "Not exactly," he said. "But do I want a chance with you?" He scanned the crowd that ebbed and flowed around them. They were standing close to a booth where women were weaving crowns of flowers and leaves to sell to festival goers. "Hell yeah I want a chance, Lucy. I would never have come all this way if I wasn't ready for something big to happen."

Lucy put her head into her hands and felt a pounding headache coming on. When she looked up again, she spoke slowly and evenly. "I can't decide whether you're being romantic or insane. I understand that Nick and I have only been dating for a few months, and that we aren't living together, we're not engaged, we have no formal commitment—"

"Exactly. If this were the Regency era, Nick and I would have every right to duel over your hand."

"Sweet lord," Lucy said, closing her eyes and keeping them shut for a long moment. "No one is brandishing a sword over my honor. That ship has long sailed anyway." A little girl in a grass skirt darted between Lucy and Dev, the dried strings of grass swishing against Lucy's bare legs as the girl ran through them. "I'm just a flawed woman who wants to love and be loved, Dev. I'm not some princess who needs a white knight."

"At our age, no one is expecting us to be without flaws, Lucy."

She looked around, unsure of what to say next. "I just don't want things to be like this."

"Like what?"

"Like *this*," she said, using both hands to gesture at their surroundings and in the direction of Nick's departure. "I've had a few very rough years, and I'm not sure I'm anyone's idea of a prize right now. I'm getting back on my feet and figuring out who I am after being married. I have a mother who needs more from me with every passing day. A business I'm just getting the hang of. And now a legal entanglement with my ex-husband and his new wife." She paused and put her hands over her eyes, breathing deeply. "It's just a lot."

"You haven't told me about the legal stuff."

Lucy pulled her hands from her eyes and waved them. "It's fine. I don't need to go into that. It's just an inheritance that we're trying to figure out since it's for both of us and we're no longer married."

"Oh, okay. I hear you," Dev said, sticking his hands into the pockets of his jeans. He'd changed out of his vacation wear and back into the uniform that Lucy knew he was most comfortable in: jeans and boots and a t-shirt. "Just know that I'm always happy to be a sounding board about whatever."

Lucy nodded. "I know. You've been great with listening and offering advice so far with these trips, and I've appreciated that a lot."

Dev looked at the ground as he kicked the dirt with the toe of his boot. "But you feel nothing for me?"

Lucy thought about this for a second. "I guess if I'm being honest, I'd say that if I felt nothing for you, I wouldn't have risked my relationship with Nick to go see the meteor shower with you that night."

That sat between them for a moment as the parade kept moving through, one band marching on and leading way to the next. The one that was currently approaching was a steel drum band, and they waited for it to pass before speaking again.

"I guess I knew that," Dev said in the relative lull between bands. "And I don't like that I'm willing to be that guy who steps in and tries to wedge himself between two other people—in fact, I didn't think I *was* that guy—but ever since you and Nick started dating, it just got to me that I didn't throw my hat in the ring sooner."

"This is hard timing for me, Dev. And I'm afraid that I'm screwing up everything here—with both of you. I don't know if Nick is serious about me going out with both of you and making some sort of decision, or if that was just his anger and exhaustion talking."

Dev shrugged. "Honestly, as a guy I would say that was probably him being literal. He really only had two choices here: pack up and leave, which he clearly doesn't want to do because he cares about you, or do the gentlemanly thing and let you make the call. I have to say I admire his tactic, and I don't know that I could do it myself. I probably would have done the stubborn thing and retreated back into my shell like the turtle I sometimes am."

"Hmmm," Lucy said, chewing on her lip. "Well. I don't think I can comfortably brush this whole thing off and enjoy the festival with you while I know that Nick is back at the resort feeling stepped on, so I think I'm just going to call it a night here and do my own thing." She pulled her crossbody purse over her chest and held it in front of herself protectively. "I'll see you tomorrow, okay?"

Lucy dashed between the float that had just passed and the next one that was coming, making it across the street just in time.

"Lucy!" Dev called after her, but she didn't hear him, and a giant float covered in feathers and carrying a huge pineapple made of flashing yellow lights came between them, blocking their view of one another as she ducked between people and disappeared into the crowd.

Chapter 15

July 4

Fiji

The drive back to the resort had been more subdued between Kona and Mindy after an evening of laughter, eating too many Fijian delicacies, and watching every cultural display they could find. With each new thing she saw, Mindy grew to love the island more and more, and with each laugh she shared with Kona, she felt herself drawn even further into his calm, centered presence.

They parked his Jeep behind the main building again and walked together down the paths that were lined with lit tiki torches. As Mindy looked up at Kona, she held onto the crown of flowers he'd gotten for her at one of the booths, touching it gently so that it wouldn't slip off her head. Around her neck was a string of hibiscus flowers, and over one arm, a canvas bag filled with items crafted on the island and made from coconut shells, bamboo, and palm fronds. She'd eagerly bought up souvenirs from every booth that supported a local charity or program, telling Kona that she wanted to take gifts back home for her children and friends. Which was true—of course a woman wouldn't go abroad without coming back laden with treasures to share—but more importantly, she felt good about filling the coffers of the programs and organizations represented by the women and men who'd made all the items.

"So," Kona said, taking her hand in his but not looking at her as they walked slowly together beneath the stars and the full moon above. "Should I walk you back to your bungalow?"

For a brief, fleeting moment Mindy panicked: should she go back? Bridger and Bagley had been inside for a couple of hours, following Dean's evening drop in to walk them, but they would be okay for a bit more; the dogs were accustomed to being inside overnight in her apartment in Manhattan. It wasn't like she walked them at three o'clock in the morning or anything. But wait—maybe Kona wanted to walk her back? Maybe he wasn't interested in inviting her back to his place. Or no! Maybe he wanted to be invited into her bungalow? Her mind raced with these thoughts and she knew she needed to land on an answer before he started to wonder whether the cat had got her tongue.

"Hey," Kona said, shaking the hand that he held in hers. "You in there?"

Mindy gave a nervous laugh. "I just...can we walk on the beach?" She held her flower crown again, looking up at him hopefully.

"You mean the beach by my place?"

Mindy nodded because she didn't trust herself to speak. She knew that—at the best of times—she rambled, and with adrenaline flooding her nervous system, she was sure that she'd talk him right out of taking her anywhere and so she kept her mouth shut and smiled.

At the fork in the path, Kona took the one that led to the beach shack, and beyond that, his bungalow. "Of course we can," he said. "As long as you're sure that's what you want to do."

Mindy nodded again.

"Can you confirm that verbally?" Kona said with a laugh. "I haven't known you long, but this is the least I've heard you talk and I'm going to need some sort of 'yes' to know that this is what you really want. Because, you know...it's the twenty-first century and a man needs explicit consent before he guides a lady onto an empty beach and back into the woods for immoral purposes."

Mindy couldn't hold in her laughter or her words any longer. "Immoral purposes!" she howled. "Oh god, it's been so long since a man had any sort of devious intentions towards me. I can't even imagine."

Kona looked at her seriously. "I can't imagine that it doesn't happen on a daily basis," he said.

"Yeah, no," Mindy said, laughing and shaking her head. "At a certain point in her life, a woman begins to feel invisible to the opposite sex. If I go out with my daughters, I end up feeling like all I am is a barrier to the men in the room who want to pounce on them." Her laughter trailed off as she realized that her words were sad—and true.

"No way," Kona said vehemently. "You're gorgeous. And full of life. The first day you walked up to my beach shack, I thought, 'Now *this* is a woman. A woman who has lived and loved, and who knows what she wants.' I was bowled over. I could hardly talk to you."

"Wait," Mindy said, stopping in her tracks. "So you were quiet the first few times we surfed because you couldn't talk to me? I made you nervous?"

"Yeah," Kona said, brow furrowed. "You did. You do. You're lovely and vibrant, and you tear through life. It's a little intimidating to a man who lives in what amounts to a shed that he built out of sticks and leaves."

"Oh, come on," Mindy said, narrowing her eyes at him. "That's an amazing house you made. It is in no way a humble little shed. And you're so...at peace. It leaves me awe-struck. I was intimidated by *you*."

They stood there, looking at one another in the light cast off by the flames of the tiki torches at the edge of the path that turned to sand and wound down to the beach.

"So," Kona said, breaking the silence that had fallen between them as they marveled at one another. "I ask again: are you sure about this?"

Mindy stepped closer to him, a smile on her face. "I am absolutely sure about this. Take me to your house. I want to. Please."

A sexy smile spread across Kona's face. "All I needed was a yes, lady. I wasn't trying to make you beg."

This made Mindy laugh again and Kona reached forward and swept her up into his strong arms, making her give a whoop of surprise as she reached up and grabbed her floral crown.

He carried her like that all the way down the path to the beach that was bathed in moonlight. When they got there, he set her back on her feet and then led her by the hand to his little house in the trees, where Kona proceeded to give Mindy the best night of her life. Finally, after years of tepid romance, and even more lukewarm attempts at physical pleasure, she was adored and attended to—for several long, languorous hours—from the top of her highlighted head to the tip of her manicured toe.

She fell asleep, tangled in Kona's bedsheets and wrapped in his thick arms, with a grin on her face and a fire in her heart.

When she woke up before sunrise, he was still holding her close.

Mindy had gotten up early and kissed a sleeping Kona goodbye so that she could get back to take her dogs out. As she walked along the totally deserted beach, the sun was just reaching its first rays into the sky, pinkening everything around her with the soft glow of morning.

She'd found Bagley and Bridger lounging peacefully in the bungalow, though they'd positioned themselves by the front door in anticipation of her arrival, and they were more than happy to get out and run free in the grass as landscapers pruned and cleared things, making it look pristine for the breakfast crowd and the early morning pool goers.

Mindy picked up after her dogs and was carrying a baggie over to the trash can while Bridger and Bagley romped and roamed, not bothering anyone, when her phone rang. She pulled it from the back pocket of her shorts: it was her son, Michael.

"Hi!" she said, putting the phone to her ear. Unlike her daughters, Michael did not prefer FaceTime. In fact, they'd tried it a few times, but an unfortunate incident whereby Michael had forgotten that there were mirrors behind him in the unfamiliar apartment where he'd spent the night with a random dating app hookup had left them both feeling uncomfortable. Mindy never again needed to see her grown son's unclothed backside, nor the front side of a naked man she didn't know as he walked into the room after a shower. From that point on, they'd stuck to phone calls.

"Mom," Michael said, sounding weary. "Why am I getting calls from Em and Shay telling me that I need to reel you back in?"

Mindy bristled. "I have no idea, Michael. As you well know, I'm a grown woman with the means to support herself from now until the end of time—several times over—and I do not need the approval of my children before I go on vacation, buy a new hat, or adopt another dog."

"Or marry our uncle," Michael added, sounding saltier than a margarita.

Mindy let the pregnant pause between them hang there; she refused to take the bait.

"Sorry, Mom," he said, not sounding particularly sorry. "I just hate when the girls call me and rant about stuff, and then I have to worry about you and what you're up to."

"Michael," Mindy said, shaking her head as Bridger came running to her, stopped at her feet, and rolled onto his back so that she could rub his belly. She kicked off her flip-flop and used her bare foot to tickle the dog's ribs. Silly canine. "You have no idea how sorry I am to interrupt your busy schedule of rotating dates and freelance writing deadlines, but—oh wait, I didn't interrupt any of that. I'm in Fiji minding my own business, and *you* are calling *me*."

"Very funny," he said, actually chuckling. "One point for Mom."

"As for what I'm up to down here, I'm busy looking for your next daddy."

"Mom," Michael said, still laughing. "You do know I'm a gay man, right? You probably don't want to tell me that you're looking for my next daddy."

"Oh! Ew!" Mindy shouted, putting a hand to her mouth. She was always doing stuff like that with her kids, committing minor gaffes that they no doubt texted one another about immediately and had a good laugh at her expense. "You know that is *not* what I meant!"

"I know, I know. That one was too easy though, Ma."

"Okay," Mindy said, putting her shoe back on as Bridger jumped up and ran off again. She watched the dogs closely to make sure they weren't getting in the way of the landscapers or bothering anyone walking up the paths. "So what can I do for you this fine morning?"

"Actually, I got a call from Paul Bleeker that I wanted to follow up on."

A dark storm cloud passed over Mindy as this news hit her. "Why in the hell would my financial advisor call you?"

"Mom," Michael said patiently. "You know that Dad and Paul go all they way back to high school."

"So?"

"Well, he probably knew better than to call Dad on your behalf, but he was worried about the sudden sale of some of your stocks and about the large gift to the Make-a-wish Foundation."

Mindy's mouth was open and her head was moving from side to side in a slow, disbelieving shake, but no words were coming out.

"Mom?" Michael said after the silence carried on. "You still there?"

"I'm here, I'm just stunned. Utterly stunned. Are we living in an episode of *Bridgerton*?"

"Sorry? You got me there, Mom. What are you getting at?"

"*Bridgerton*. The Regency era drama on Netflix where the women are property to be married off. They don't have any rights, any finances of their own, or any say in how their lives go. Is that me?" Mindy could feel her blood pressure rising along with her voice. "Is it, Michael? Am I, the person who brought all the money into our family via my own family's business acumen, completely without the right to manage *my money* as I see fit? Not to mention my life? I can marry whomever I want, spend my money as I choose, and decide whether or not to serve every acquaintance I have up on a silver platter to my pampered daughter so that she can use it for her own gain at work. And none of you has the right to say *a damn thing about it.*"

"Mom—" Michael interjected, sounding tired.

"Nope. I'm done here." Mindy whistled for her dogs and they came running in her direction. "I have plans today, and I'm not going to sit here and be lectured by my thirty-year-old son. And you can tell your sisters not to bother calling me for the next few days either, because guess what? Mama's off duty." Mindy bent forward and clipped the leashes on her dogs. "Sayonara, happy trails, hasta la vista, kids," she said, ending the call and shoving her phone back into her pocket. It felt good. Amazing, actually.

No sooner had she started to walk when the phone rang again. Mindy took a deep breath and yanked it out of her pocket, expecting it to be her son calling back. Instead, it was an unfamiliar number.

"Hello?"

"Why did you leave?"

"Oh," Mindy said, flushing. It was Kona. "I needed to walk my dogs."

"Tonight you should bring them here with you."

The flush turned into a bright red burn that crawled all over her skin and made the roots of her hair tingle. "Tonight?"

"Unless you have other plans...but you did leave a sticky note on my bathroom mirror this morning with your phone number on it, so I was assuming you wanted me to call and invite you back."

A big, goofy grin spread over Mindy's face. "Yeah, I want to come back. But hey, aren't we doing a surf lesson in like thirty minutes?"

She glanced at her watch as she let the dogs drag her back down the wooden walkway to her bungalow.

"Oh, are we still pretending to surf together?"

"Stop!" Mindy laughed. "I was really getting the hang of it and I want to learn!"

Kona grew serious. "Hey, then we'll keep surfing. I'm only teasing anyway. I would never try to convince a woman not to pursue her interests. Please know that."

"I know, I know. Let me feed the dogs and change into a bikini and I'll meet you at the beach, okay?"

"It's a deal."

Thirty minutes later, Mindy was in the water, stomach on the surfboard, paddling into the waves. She already felt a thousand times more confident than she had the first day Kona had taken her into the water, and while she would never leave the island being able to say that she was a surfer girl, there was pride for her in the knowledge that she'd fearlessly taken on something that she'd never even considered trying.

After a few trips out into the water, a few subsequent falls, and much cheering from Kona, Mindy dragged her board in with a happy smile on her face.

"You're really getting the hang of this," Kona said, arms folded across his bare chest as he watched her from a spot on the sand where the water barely broke at his ankles. He never took his eyes off of her, though he'd grown gradually more hands-off with each passing day, offering pointers and comments and always standing at the ready in case she needed him, but not treating her nearly so much like a pampered New York woman who needed a constant chaperone in the ocean.

"I actually feel like I'm getting it!" Mindy shouted as the waves crashed and sprayed the backs of her thighs.

"It reminds me of when I taught my daughter to surf," Kona said, a warm smile in his eyes.

Mindy stopped cold. "Your daughter?"

"Yeah," Kona said. "My daughter Phaedra. She's twenty-four."

"You never told me you had children," Mindy said, hating that her voice sounded accusing. Her smile faded. "I had no idea."

Kona shrugged. "I only have one child, and I'm telling you about her now."

"Where is she? On the island?"

Kona gave a single nod. "She lives here. Went to New Zealand for a few years to work as an au pair and take some college courses, and now she lives in an apartment with her boyfriend and works at the Chamber of Commerce."

"I just..." Mindy felt like she should have known about Phaedra. Not that it was necessary for people to exchange every personal detail with a one-night stand, though it wasn't as if she'd ever actually *had* any one-night stands. And Kona was not the kind of man you spent a night with and then slunk away from in the morning with no plans to see him again. No judgment as far as other people were concerned, but that just wasn't her style. Maybe it was okay to spend a night with a person and not have told each other things like that yet, but she was confused about why he wouldn't have mentioned his daughter when she'd told him straight away about her three kids, and she suddenly felt like a college girl who'd just found out that the guy she'd slept with after a party was someone she barely knew.

Kona was watching her face. "I'm sorry, I should have told you about her. I'm kind of slow to open up about my life. I've always been that way."

Mindy looked at her feet as the water from her wet hair dripped onto her forehead and ran down her temples. "I want to know more about you," she said, looking up at him through her lashes. "I want to know who you are."

"I've just told you more than I tell about ninety percent of the people I meet." Kona unfolded his arms and reached for her surfboard, taking it easily under one arm and then offering her his other hand. "Let's get you up to the beach shack to dry off. You look cold."

Mindy's teeth had started to chatter, though she wasn't sure if it was from the cold water or from her nerves.

"What about you? I know you have three kids, but I don't even know what you do for work. Or, sorry—if you work? I know you're divorced."

"Twice," Mindy said, still holding his hand as they walked. "I was married to my college sweetheart, and then after we divorced I...well, there's no great way to say this: I married his brother."

Kona stopped walking and turned his head to look at her. "You married his brother?"

"Is that judgment or awe I hear in your voice?"

"I think that's definitely awe," Kona said. "Nothing sticks it to a man like marrying his brother."

"Younger brother," Mindy added for maximum effect. "Arthur is ten years younger than Kevin."

Kona put a fist to his mouth and coughed out a laugh. "Whoa. You insulted his manhood."

Mindy lifted an eyebrow lazily. "He deserved it. He insulted my womanhood."

"Well played."

Mindy was warming up as they walked, and so she kept going. "And as for what I do for work, I sit on the board of my family business, which is Shulnuts Donuts. I'm not sure if you've heard of them as we don't have any in Fiji—"

Kona was still standing in the same spot, now openly gaping at her. "I've been to New York. I know Shulnuts. Wait—Mindy Shultz?"

She nodded, smiling at him because it pleased her to know that Kona had been to one of her family's shops.

Kona let go of her hand and set the surfboard on the sand. A lean couple ran by them in jogging shorts and matching baseball caps, not speaking to one another as they sprinted up the beach. Kona ignored them and narrowed his eyes at Mindy.

"So wait," he said, running one hand over his mouth. "Are you telling me that you're a—and forgive me, because I don't know the politically correct way of saying this—you're a *millionaire?* Or something along those lines?"

Mindy was still smiling, but she could feel it morph from a genuine, happy grin to the somewhat less sincere, guarded one she used when talking to someone about something that made her uncomfortable.

"In a manner of speaking, yes," she said, lacing her fingers together in front of her. "My family has worked hard for decades, and the company has done well."

Kona glanced up and down the beach. It was his turn to look confused. "So then what are you doing with me?"

Mindy frowned. "What do you mean?"

He looked pained to even have to put it into words, but he did it anyway. "Is this just some vacation fling with the hired help?" he asked, his voice raspy.

"What? Kona—no," Mindy said, her breath catching in her throat. She unlaced her hands and took the two steps between them, putting her palms against his bare chest. "No way. I like you. I'm not some rich girl who just buys people, or whatever it is you're thinking. Please don't assume anything about me."

"That's just a lot to process," he said, looking down into her eyes with his normally crystal clear blue ones. They'd gone cloudy with his thoughts, and Mindy wanted nothing more than to reach up and put her hands on both sides of his face, to reassure him, to let him know that she *was* exactly who he thought she was and not some woman who only lived for money.

"You can process it," she said. "We're both finding out things about each other. And I still have more questions too, like—are you divorced? Or were you never married to Phaedra's mom?"

"Divorced," he said, his eyes still darker than usual as he stared at her. "Her mother and I met and married in Sydney, and we split up when Phaedra was four. I've been mostly single since then."

"So you didn't marry her sister out of spite?" Mindy joked, hoping for levity.

The best she got was a half smile. "No, I didn't go that route."

They were quiet for a minute as the water lapped up onto the shore and rolled back out. "Can I still come over tonight?" Mindy asked. "Bring the dogs?"

Kona searched her eyes. "Of course you can. I want you to."

Mindy nodded, biting on her lower lip. "Okay," she said softly. "Then I will. But hey," she said, her hands still on his chest. "You've got customers standing outside the shack there." She nodded at a family in board shorts as they stood there, waiting for Kona. He turned and glanced at them, giving a small wave.

"I should go," he said. "I'll see you this evening?"

Mindy nodded and then took a step back, watching as he walked up the beach to help the people who were waiting there. She shielded her eyes with her hands, admiring his strong figure, his surefooted, confident walk. Kona wasn't someone she was willing to walk away from over a few details that they'd both been reticent to share.

In fact, after only knowing him a handful of days, she wasn't sure how she'd be able to walk away from him at all.

Chapter 16

July 5

Fiji

Lucy rolled over the minute her eyes opened and looked around the room expectantly. No Nick.

She'd come in the night before hoping to catch him awake, but he'd been stretched out on the couch with his face pressed into the back cushions, and she had known better than to wake him. Now, the couch was perfectly made up, and the blanket he'd covered himself with was folded on one end, his pillow resting on top of it.

Lucy rushed around the bungalow, looking for signs of him. The bathroom was empty. The small deck held nothing but the lounge chairs. She stood there for a moment, looking out at the water and wondering how she'd gotten there. Things had been going so well between her and Nick, and as far as she could tell, she and Dev were just friends with a slight edge. This never had to happen, and she wanted desperately to believe that she hadn't encouraged this in any way.

Except...there was that moonlit motorcycle ride. Lucy put her hands to her head and held it tightly like she was trying to squeeze away a hangover. Except she wasn't. She hadn't had anything to drink the night before, and this was definitely a tension headache that threatened to balloon as the day went on.

She'd lain in bed in the darkness the night before, staying quiet so as not to bother Nick, as she messaged Carmen and Bree, the friends she'd met on the trip to Venice for Valentine's Day. The two women had come along on the journey with the Holiday Adventure Club as a way for Bree to get back out there after the tragic death of her young husband, and the three of them had hit it off. Carmen and Bree were the first girlfriends Lucy had made in ages, and their group chat had been a part of her life since February, filling her life with laughter and the kind of kinship that only comes from other women friends.

Lucy walked back into the bungalow and picked up her phone from the nightstand next to the bed.

This is SOMETHING ELSE, Carmen had written the night before. *Nick expects you to date them both? What is this, "The Bachelor"?*

Yeah, I'm not into this, Bree agreed. *I think it's weird. Nick should have punched Dev.*

Lucy re-read the messages, shaking her head as she did. She knew Bree was being overly dramatic on purpose; no one wanted anyone to get into a physical altercation at her expense.

I don't know...seems like this could be an opportunity, Carmen said.

It's more like a nightmare, you guys, Lucy added. *I'm hurting Nick no matter what I do, and it's made things awkward with Dev. How are the three of us ever going to go back to our normal interactions when we get home?*

Carmen piped up first: *You're probably not, tbh. This trip is going to change everything, whether you like it or not.*

I like it NOT, Lucy said definitively. *And all of this is on top of the nonsense with my ex-husband. I feel like it's too much to handle all at once.*

What's up with him, btw? (From Bree.)

He wants to reconvene with the mediator when I get back home. I've got downtime between this trip and the next, which isn't until Labor Day. So I don't know. Not looking forward to it.

Where is the trip for Labor Day again? Bree asked.

Lisbon.

Ooooh. I feel like I'm due for another vacation, Carmen said. *Is there still room for us to join?*

Don't tease me, you two. I'd love to have you there!

Lucy skimmed all the messages from the night before as she stood there in her t-shirt and underwear, hair messy, chewing on her thumbnail. Having Carmen and Bree join her on a trip again *would* be amazing, but at the moment she really needed to find Nick.

She was about to set her phone down when a text came through —this time from Dev: *Hey, I know you need to take some time today and do what you've gotta do. I'm here though.*

Lucy's fingers hovered over the keyboard as she thought of a response, but rather than sending anything, she tossed the phone onto the bed and went to take a shower.

* * *

There was no sign of Nick anywhere, though his bags were still in the bungalow, so she knew he hadn't taken off. Lucy had tried texting and calling him, but to no avail. So after a fast shower, she'd thrown on a pair of shorts and a tank top, braided her wet hair, and put on mascara before rushing down the wooden planks and past the other bungalows.

As she walked, her eyes scanned the grass, the open restaurants, and the paths around her. No Nick. Lucy walked through the sliding doors of the main building with purpose, striding up to the front counter and placing her elbows on it as she waited, somewhat impatiently, for Jasmine to finish the call she was on.

Finally, she turned to Lucy with a smile. "Good morning."

"Hi, Jasmine. Is there a message for me by any chance?"

"Yes, there is," she said smoothly, her smile not quite reaching her eyes. In that instant, Lucy felt that Jasmine—while acting completely professional—was judging the whole scene that had gone down the day before right there in the lobby, and most likely she was siding with Nick, the obviously wounded party.

Lucy's eyes fell to the counter and she tried not to feel the shame that washed over her as Jasmine slid an envelope over to her. Her name was scrawled on the front in Nick's handwriting.

"Thank you," she said, walking away with the envelope in hand. Her flip-flops slapped against the floors and Lucy tried to step lightly to make herself less of a spectacle.

Outside, she ripped into the envelope and pulled out a piece of paper that had been folded into thirds. *I'll be at the dock at nine-thirty. We're booked on a boat cruise for breakfast, so just show up. Here's your ticket.*

Lucy unfolded the last section of the paper and a ticket slid into her hand. She glanced at her watch: 9:21. Slim margins.

She took off at a fast clip in the direction of the dock where she knew that boats launched from, and as she rushed past tired-looking parents carting pool towels, floaties, toddlers, and paper cups of coffee, all she could think about was that if she screwed this up with Nick, he'd take his already packed suitcases and leave. She looked at her watch: 9:24. Lucy took off her flip-flops and held them in her hand as she broke into a run, cutting across the grass to avoid the people walking on the paths.

She leapt—actually took a flying dancer's leap and soared—over a giant hose that a landscaper had dragged across a path as he watered a huge bed of flowers. Nothing would stop her from getting across the resort in time to make this boat, and she picked up the pace as she rounded a bend. She was almost there.

Ahead, the trees cleared and the path dropped away as a dock appeared. Lucy slowed down and stopped for a second to catch her breath. 9:28. She'd made it. She slipped her flip-flops back on and wiped stray hairs from her sweaty forehead as she approached the boat calmly, trying to act like she hadn't just run a mini-marathon in record time so that her boyfriend wouldn't give up on her entirely and leave her on Fiji.

"Ticket?" a young woman in khaki shorts and a white t-shirt with a name tag asked, holding out her hand with a friendly smile.

"Yes," Lucy said, thrusting the envelope at her with the note and the ticket inside. "Oh, sorry." With shaking hands, she fished the ticket out and handed it over, keeping the envelope for herself. "I'm meeting someone here."

The woman looked at Lucy's ticket and then pulled out a neon pink wristband, which she snapped around Lucy's wrist. "Your table is on the top deck, number twelve," she said, pointing at a polished staircase just inside the boat. "Your party is already waiting."

Lucy's heart was still racing from the exertion and from the fear that she might miss the boat, but she held onto the handrail and ascended the stairs, eyes wide as she looked for Nick.

He was sitting at a table by the railing of the boat, face turned to the water, a cup of coffee on a saucer in front of him. There were only twelve tables up there, and each was covered by a white table-cloth that had been set with coffee cups and silverware.

"Hi," Lucy said, still breathless. She slid into the chair across from him and he turned to look at her.

"I wasn't sure you were going to make it," he said, searching her face.

"I wish you would have woken me up. Or texted me. It was a lucky guess to check the front desk."

Nick shrugged. "You're an intelligent woman. I figured you'd find me if you wanted to." It came out like a challenge. A dare.

"Coffee?" A man in the same khaki shorts and white-t-shirt uniform as the woman on the dock was standing at their table with a carafe in one hand.

"Oh, yes please," Lucy said, waiting as he turned over her cup and filled it. "Thank you."

The boat slipped from its place at the dock smoothly, and they started to move into the open water.

"Where are we headed?" Lucy asked, taking her first grateful sip of coffee.

"South Sea Island," Nick said, smiling for the first time since she'd sat down. "It's like its own little resort. Food, entertainment—it's all there."

Lucy set her cup down and it rattled the saucer. "Oh! How long is this adventure?"

"Eight hours," Nick said, narrowing his eyes. "Is that a problem? Do you have other plans?"

Lucy swallowed carefully before she spoke. "Nope. I'm all yours."

The words hung between them for a moment and then Nick nodded and looked out at the water, breathing in the sea air as the wind ruffled his hair. "I want to believe that," he said quietly, not looking at Lucy.

"Then you should."

The waiter reappeared, hands clasped behind his back. "The breakfast buffet is open on the lower deck," he said. "Please feel free to visit it as many times as you'd like while we make our way to South Sea Island." With a slight bow, he moved on to deliver his message to the next table.

Neither Lucy or Nick made a move to stand up.

"Did you hear me?" she implored, still watching his profile. "I didn't ask him to come here. And last night after you left, we talked for a few minutes and then I came back to the resort."

"You didn't have to," Nick said, finally looking her directly in the eye. "I fully expected you to stay out and have fun."

"Nick, come on," Lucy said, reaching across the table and putting her hand on his forearm. "You can't really believe that I would stay out and have some great time when you'd just dropped a bomb like that."

Nick didn't look away. "I wasn't trying to drop a bomb, Lucy. I'm just trying to protect my heart here. I was all in on this, and I just feel like you're not."

Lucy shook her head. "I don't know why you feel that way," she said, though as the words came out of her mouth, she could feel that they were somewhat disingenuous. "I'm in this too, Nick, and you've been amazing. Going to Buffalo to help me with my mom, coming with me to St. Barts, racing down here to make sure things are good between us—who else would do those things?"

"Any man who understands what he's got would do the same," Nick said quickly, his eyes flashing. "Listen," he said, changing courses. "Let's go get some breakfast, yeah? I feel like we both skipped dinner last night, and this day is going to go downhill fast if we're both tired and hungry."

"Agreed," Lucy said, standing.

They made their way down to the long buffet table that ran along one side of the boat on the lower deck. Servers in white aprons and white chefs hats stood behind the chafing dishes as steam curled up from the piles of freshly made waffles, scrambled eggs, and crispy bacon. Lucy picked up a plate and when she'd reached the end of the table, she had a stack of three Belgian waffles covered in bright red strawberries and rich whipped cream. In her other hand was a smaller plate with bacon, eggs, and sausages. She carried them carefully up the stairs and sat down again, waiting politely for Nick to return before she picked up her fork.

"Impressive," he said, setting down his omelette and a glass of fresh-squeezed grapefruit juice. "If you don't finish that, I'd be happy to help."

Lucy picked up her silverware. "This is beautiful, Nick. Thank you for getting us on this boat."

Nick cut into his omelette. Cheese and sautéed mushrooms oozed onto his plate. "I hope I'm not keeping you from anything. It was probably wrong of me to book your entire day up without warning." He glanced up at her with just his eyes as he focused on getting the first bite of omelette onto his fork.

Lucy chose to steer clear of his obvious meaning and stay right in the center of her lane. "No, I'm good," she said with a smile, cutting off a piece of her waffle. "Everyone in the tour group is either doing individual things today like kayaking or hanging out at the beach, and I'm sure some will head back to the Bula Festival to see what's happening there during the day."

"Mmm," Nick said, chewing. He washed down his omelette with a sip of grapefruit juice. "Lucky for me."

They smiled at each other carefully and continued eating. Lucy closed her eyes and turned her face up to the morning sun as they cut across the water. South Sea Island was visible on the horizon, and she was getting full and caffeinated and feeling much better about everything. Maybe it was the distance that they were currently putting between Nick and Dev by spending the day off the resort, but for a second Lucy was able to pretend that this was just like being on St. Barts with Nick, and that there was no drama or anything to interrupt their time together. She opened her eyes and looked around. She was going to have a good day, and she'd make sure that Nick did too. He deserved that.

* * *

Spencer sat on the bottom deck of the boat with a plate of fruit and cheese and a cup of coffee in front of her on the tiny table. She'd convinced Heinrich that she wasn't feeling well that day, and he'd easily waved her off, assuming that she'd spend the day in bed or perhaps getting a massage at the spa.

Instead, she'd followed Nick to the front desk and then bought herself a ticket on this boat excursion after hearing him purchase two tickets and request to leave one at the front counter for Lucy.

It was just a hunch on her part—she really wasn't sure that anything of interest would happen on South Sea Island—but she'd always had a nose for news, and aside from the Mindy Shultz/Dreamy Island Guy drama, watching this love triangle implode with the travel agency owner had been high on Spencer's list of potentially show-worthy scenarios.

When Nick and Lucy had come down the stairs to hit the buffet Spencer had turned her back and stared out at the water, and now that they were getting close to docking at the island and disembarking, she knew that all she'd have to do was put on her oversized hat and a pair of sunglasses and blend in with the other women who'd come to South Sea Island for a day of sun and relaxation.

Sure enough, a group of college-age girls who didn't look that much younger than Spencer were there to celebrate someone's twenty-first birthday, so she glommed on to the tail end of their group, holding her Lilly Pulitzer tote bag over one shoulder and laughing along with the rest of the girls as they climbed off the boat and made their way onto the island.

Right at the end of the dock was a long wooden "Welcome to South Sea Island" sign with letters that looked like they'd been branded onto the wood with a hot iron. Spencer turned on her hand-held camera and started recording; it was never wrong to get filler footage, and Fiji was certainly providing her with a lot of gorgeous scenery and interesting shots that she could use later.

Just beyond the welcome sign was a row of women sitting on the sand, smiling widely and waving at the visitors as they trekked up onto the beach. The women were dressed in matching cap-sleeved blue shirts and skirts printed with a wave pattern that was reminiscent of the ocean. On their heads and wrists were matching wreathes of green foliage. Other people were shooting video with their phones, so Spencer did a long shot of the women with sunlight filtering into their dark hair through the palm trees overhead. She knew she was getting some good stuff and Lucy and her man weren't even off the boat yet.

Spencer followed the twenty-first birthday group all the way to the bar, which was really just a wraparound counter underneath a dried grass roof. The young women all piled up to the bar and started ordering drinks, and Spencer looked around, hoping for a good place to park herself while she waited for Lucy and Nick. Her payoff came quickly, as the two of them came strolling up the boardwalk looking subdued just a few minutes later. Nick pointed in the direction of the beach and Lucy nodded, so they turned left at one of those direction signs that had multiple handmade signs nailed to it that tell the distance from that point to somewhere else. Normally the boards say things like how many miles to Cuba or New York City or Jamaica, but this one had signs that pointed this way and that for the bar, for kayak rentals, and for beach amenities.

Spencer followed at a safe distance, hidden behind her hat and sunglasses. Nick stopped off at a little hut to pay for two chairs and an umbrella, and Spencer waited until they were done, then quickly slapped down her money and rented a chair for herself.

Luckily it was still early and much of the beach was empty, so it was easy for her to choose a chair in the row right behind Nick and Lucy. Spencer spread out her towel without making any noise and then settled in, camera resting on the chair next to her left hip. She laid out flat on her back and closed her eyes, pretending to be absorbed in her thoughts or working on her tan, when in truth, she already had her ears tuned in to their conversation.

"So," Nick was saying, turning their chairs just slightly so that they were out of the sun. "Any word on the inheritance?"

"Is this your way of telling me that you're only with me for my big money?" Lucy joked, kicking off her flip-flops and laying on her stomach with her face turned toward Nick. A bikini string poked out from under her tank top, but she kept her street clothes on for the time being, stretching out beneath the umbrella as she chatted with Nick.

"Very funny," he said, looking at her like he normally might have laughed at that joke, but there was some sort of tension that had dimmed the humor for him.

Spencer slowly and gently lifted her camera and set it on her stomach, pointing the lens at Lucy and Nick, visible between their two lounge chairs. She turned it on and started to record.

"There's nothing major going on, though," Lucy said, closing her eyes as she rested her chin on her hands. Next to her, Nick had laid on his back, one knee pulled up as he faced the water. "Jason and his wife still want me to relinquish my part of the inheritance, which frankly, I think is bull. I had a fabulous relationship with his Aunt Marion, and I don't see any reason why I'm not entitled to accept her gift."

"And yet he still disagrees?"

Lucy lifted one shoulder but didn't bother to open her eyes behind her sunglasses. "I guess not. He thinks that he and the new wife deserve to be in charge of the buildings, and so we've agreed to disagree. And we continue trying to have our attorneys mediate this process and come up with a reasonable plan that satisfies us all."

"Do you think it made it worse that his aunt left you a larger share than she left to him?"

"Oh, hands down. He has to hate that. Jason is nothing if not a prideful man who feels that he deserves everything and then some. No offense to your people—I'm not trying to say that all men are as self-involved as he is."

"None taken," Nick said, turning his head so that Spencer caught him in profile. The morning sun was lighting up the beach in front of them, and the shot was perfect, as was the sound. She wasn't sure how much of this conversation she'd be able to use in her footage, given the private nature of the lawsuit or inheritance or whatever they were talking about, but on a personal level, she found the situation pretty fascinating.

"The whole thing is making it that much harder to put my divorce behind me," Lucy said, rolling over onto her back and putting one arm behind her head. "I honestly prefer not having to talk to Jason, to see him, or even to think about him. I mean," she said, turning her head quickly so that she was looking at Nick, "don't get me wrong—I'm not having any feelings for him because I'm being forced to see him—I'm just happier and I do better when I can pretend he never even existed."

Nick nodded, looking out at the beach thoughtfully. After a moment, he spoke up. "I would say the same about Laura, but I don't mind when something comes up that forces me to think about her." Lucy reached out a hand and put it on Nick's arm; in turn, he slid her palm into his hand and held it. "But then we never married or went through an acrimonious divorce. We simply lost a child together."

"Oh, Nick," Lucy said.

"I know I don't talk about Daisy a lot," he said, still holding Lucy's hand. "And I'm not talking about her now to play on your sympathies, I'm just saying that I get it. Some memories are hard to dig up. Some things you wish you could let go. But life is this giant patchwork of love, and loss, and experience, and ultimately it all adds up to make us who we are."

They sat there quietly, fingers interlaced, faces pointed at the water as the sun brushed the sand beyond their chairs.

"I like who you are, Nick Epperson," Lucy said hoarsely. "And I'm sorry if I ever made you feel like I didn't. Everything is just so complicated sometimes, you know?"

Nick nodded. "I do."

"And I just want it to be easy."

"But it's not."

"No, it's not," Lucy agreed.

They stayed silent for a while. "So how about if we just enjoy the beach for the day?"

"I can do that," Lucy said, giving his hand a tug. "Hey, want a piña colada?"

"I thought you'd never ask," Nick said, holding up his hand as a waitress in short black shorts and a South Sea Island t-shirt walked by with a tray in her hand.

It was then that Spencer turned off her camera. Nick had lost a child, Lucy had suffered what was obviously a painful divorce, and they were clearly in the midst of some sort of uncomfortable love triangle; it was time for Spencer to back off. She didn't mind some of the drama and she was sure her idea was a solid one, but for the time being, she felt like the right thing to do was to retreat.

Without disrupting them, she put her camera into her tote bag, gathered her things, and headed back to the bar. Maybe that group of twenty-one year olds had some stories to tell, and maybe if she bought them a round of drinks they'd dish some dirt with her.

After all, everyone had a story, and it was all about figuring out the angle as you tried to find it.

Chapter 17

July 5

Fiji

When Spencer got back to the bungalow late that afternoon, Heinrich was waiting. He sat on the deck with a bottle of beer in hand, one ankle crossed over the opposite knee.

"What are you up to?" he asked her plainly, putting the bottle to his mouth and taking a swig.

The sun was dropping behind Spencer, and it touched her bare shoulders as she faced Heinrich. She looked beautiful in that golden light, with her hair a bit wild, her skin warm and tanned.

"It's nothing bad," she said.

"You told me you were sick, so I took a break this afternoon to come back and check on you. It looks like a maid came through in the morning and nothing has been touched since. So I'll ask again, what are you up to?"

Spencer set down her tote bag and then went to sit at the foot of Heinrich's lounge chair. "Okay," she said, "hear me out before you lose it—promise?"

"I make no promises." Heinrich felt much as he had when his oldest daughter had taken his Porsche out for a joy ride without permission and gotten her first speeding ticket. The comparison alone made his heart sink even further. In this moment was he really feeling toward Spencer the same way he'd felt toward his daughter Emily nearly twenty years ago?

"I've been working on a side project," Spencer said, forging ahead without waiting for him to say anything more. "I told you that I thought there was more going on here at this resort than we were capturing, so I've been getting footage of other scenarios."

"I heard from Bill Pullman," he said, letting the name drop and sink like a coin tossed in a fountain. "I'm aware of the side project."

Spencer blinked slowly. Heinrich had no idea why she'd imagined that her reaching out to the network would be confidential, but clearly she had. Heinrich and Bill Pullman had been working together for nearly thirty years; there was no way Bill *wouldn't* let him know that one of his crew was operating independently. And he had to admit, the phone call had caught him off guard, but he hadn't been as surprised as he might have imagined he'd be. Spencer was a go-getter. Whip-smart and curious as a cat. There was no way she'd be happy forever running errands and assisting people on set. He knew that.

"Tell me more," Heinrich prompted.

Spencer cleared her throat and leaned over, reaching for her bag. From it, she pulled the handheld camera. "There are a few mini-dramas playing out here at the resort that I thought might make for good television."

She fiddled with the camera for a minute and then pulled up an image on its tiny screen. There, in perfect light, sat Nick and Lucy (whose names Heinrich did not yet know), holding hands with the glittering water visible between them in the distance.

Heinrich could already feel himself preparing for her pitch. He might be perturbed that she'd gone off and done something without his blessing, but Heinrich was—at heart—a tv man. And he knew good television when he saw it.

"I'm all ears," he said. "Give me what you've got."

* * *

Lucy and Nick stepped off the boat and back onto the resort property around five-thirty that evening. They were tired and happy after a day of sun, splashing in the clear-as-glass water around South Sea Island, and drinking piña coladas while they'd talked about life.

The day-long excursion had included a full barbecue, so they'd loaded up their plates with chicken palau; ceviche made from mahi mahi, cucumbers, onions, and coconut cream; fries with garlic butter; and cassava cake, a savory dessert topped with sweet cream. After that, they'd napped on their umbrella-covered lounge chairs, then awoken to a dance performance by a group of men in the customary dried grass skirts and face paint. At some point during the day, Lucy had even forgotten that she had people back at the resort who might be looking for her with questions. In her rush, she'd left her phone in her bungalow, but by the time she'd fallen asleep under the umbrella, she didn't miss it at all.

"Thank you again for planning that," Lucy said, winding her fingers through Nick's as they walked across the resort grounds. A few sprinklers had kicked on and the early evening sunlight caught the droplets of water, creating little rainbows and showers of golden glitter. The entire day felt like a postcard.

"I had a good time," Nick said, pulling her fingers into his and holding them firmly. "I don't want to let you go this evening."

"I'm not—" Lucy said, honestly confused for a second about why he might be letting her go. But then she remembered: Dev. There was no way to avoid him after vanishing all day.

"It's okay," Nick said, looking at the ground as they walked. "I'm not trying to push you into his arms, and in fact, it will break my heart if you end up there, but I need you to be sure, Lucy. I can't have you with me back at home, but still wondering about what you might have missed with him."

"Nick," she said, tilting her head as she watched him.

"No, I'm serious. This isn't high school, and I know that. We're almost forty years old. This is how life works."

Lucy stayed quiet as they walked on.

"Things are never going to be perfect," Nick said gently. "But they should be good. They should feel right—to both of us."

"I hear you."

He squeezed her hand as they wound past the other bungalows on the wooden walkway. "Why don't you head in and change or do what you have to do. I'm going to take a walk." He stopped and turned to face Lucy, the slightest hint of uncertainty in his eyes. "Thanks for coming with me today."

Lucy lifted her chin as Nick lowered his head. He kissed her gently. She could feel tears prick at the back of her eyes and she wanted to squelch them; this was not the time to give in to her own emotions.

Rather than say something small like "See you later," or "I won't be late," or anything that even hinted at the fact that she'd most likely be out with Dev for a while, Lucy put her hands on Nick's shoulders and pulled him close to kiss him again.

Once, twice, and then a third time for good measure.

* * *

"So," Dev said, pulling out Lucy's chair and waiting for her to sit. "I was worried I'd lost you today."

Lucy was tempted to say *But you never had me*, only she knew what he meant so she just smiled and took the napkin from the table and spread it over her lap.

Dev had texted her a number of times throughout the day while her phone lay on the bed in her bungalow, and when she'd walked back in, her screen was already lit up by an incoming call from him.

He'd taken it upon himself to create a whole romantic dinner for them, and now Lucy sat there on a secluded section of the beach just beyond one of the resort's restaurants as two servers disappeared and reappeared with various items that they served and presented.

"I'm sorry about today," Lucy said, pausing as the waiter poured a glass of champagne for each of them. "Nick didn't tell me that we'd be on a boat cruise for eight hours, otherwise I would have brought my phone along and let you know."

"It's no problem," Dev said smoothly, sidestepping any comment on Nick's having taken her off the radar for the day.

They sat there for a moment, watching as two seagulls swooped and dove into the water, the sky a pastel backdrop behind them. Lucy looked up at the palm trees that towered over them; someone had wound the trees with clear twinkling lights, and all along the sand from the path down to their table were hurricane lamps filled with lit candles.

"Cheers," Lucy said, picking up her champagne glass. "And thank you for this—it's lovely."

Dev suddenly looked shy. "It's not really my style, as I'm sure you can imagine," he said. "But even though I come across like some sort of greasy rock 'n' roller, I clean up alright." He glanced down at the button-up shirt that he wore with a pair of black dress pants—not jeans this time.

"I never doubted it for a second," Lucy said, feeling a swirl of anxious energy in her stomach that she tried to quell with two quick sips of champagne. The bubbles went right to her head and she smiled gratefully at a waitress who appeared with a bread basket. "And for the record," she said to Dev, "I like your usual look. It suits you. But this looks great too."

They each took a piece of bread and buttered it as a candle flickered between them on the table. It was strange because they knew each other well enough to banter on a daily basis back home, but now suddenly in this formal setting, they were acting like two nervous teenagers at the prom.

"Anyway," Dev said at the same time that Lucy said, "So tell me about—"

They both laughed and gestured for the other to go first.

"Okay," Lucy said. "I was just going to say that I wanted to hear more about your parents and your family. They're running the coffee shop this week, and I don't really know anything about them."

Dev picked up his champagne flute. "Uh, they're cool," he said. "I've got a sister who lives in Jamaica, which is where my mom is from. Layla. She's thirty-one, has three little boys. Hellions—all of them." He smiled fondly, clearly imagining his nephews. "My dad is from Mexico. He moved to Florida with his parents when he was a teenager, spoke no English, and ended up starting his own business in his twenties. He's been successful."

"What kind of business?"

"He started out cleaning pools in Tampa, then at some point he'd saved enough money to buy the company. Don't ask me how; I think the world must have been a different place in the eighties."

"Completely different," Lucy agreed. "My mom hasn't worked since before I was born, and yet she managed to buy a house on two acres and live reasonably well on alimony from my dad and a small— very small—amount of money that she got when her parents passed away."

"Amazing, isn't it?" Dev shook his head. "I've taken out some sizable loans to make my business happen, and I'm still renting a house in my mid-thirties because I'm trying to sink all my money into my coffee shop. And here are my parents, living the life."

"And your mom—what does she do?"

"She was a bookkeeper when my dad hired her to work for him almost forty years ago, and they fell in love because she was the only one in the office who could make my dad a decent cup of coffee, according to the story they always tell."

"That's sweet," Lucy said, taking another bite of her bread and butter.

"My favorite part of the story is that my dad decided to branch out from cleaning pools and start offering custom builds. He'd done enough pool maintenance at that point to know what people wanted, and before he knew it, he was designing and building outdoor living spaces for construction companies. He and my mom sold the business and retired a year or two ago."

"That's incredible," Lucy said, leaning back as a waiter appeared with colorful three-tomato salads drizzled with a honey-citrus dressing. "I admire that so much."

"Yeah, my parents are the center of our family," Dev said, spearing a tomato with his fork. "When I started my business, they were my role models and advisors."

"No wonder you're so good at giving business advice." When she'd been in the midst of planning the trip to Venice, Dev's suggestions had been invaluable.

He smiled as he chewed. "Actually, I'm just interested in advertising and marketing in general, and it seemed like you needed a little help to get things off the ground."

Lucy blushed. "Well, you had ideas when I was flailing around, so thank you."

They talked about his upbringing in Tampa, his first motorcycle, and why Lucy had gone into medicine as they finished their salads and the main course arrived. No one had asked Lucy what she wanted, but she didn't mind at all when she was presented with a plate of Fijian coconut fish with tomatoes, spinach, and rice.

"So you felt that helpless when it came to your mother?" Dev asked, cutting into his flaky fish.

"I did. Absolutely. I spent my teenage years trying to understand and to help her—not to mention trying to get by socially—and I felt like if I became a doctor, maybe I could actually do something for her."

"And yet, rather than go into—what? Psychology? Psychiatry? Elder care?—you ended up doing autopsies?" He looked at her with curiosity as he took a bite of fish.

"Well," Lucy said. She picked up the white wine that the waiter had poured with their main course. "In medical school I fell in love with forensics. I think it's sort of like when you find the right person, you know? You don't care if it makes perfect sense, and you definitely don't care whether it makes other people happy, you just know it's what makes *you* happy."

Dev had set down his fork and was watching her, elbows on the table, fingers laced together under his chin. "And so now that we're talking about love, *are* you happy? Is Nick the one?"

Lucy put down her wine glass and looked out at the water. The sun was tucked halfway into the horizon and it flared in the sky like a beacon sending a signal, encouraging Lucy to speak her truth.

"I don't know," she whispered, surprised as the words crossed her lips. She'd expected her own answer to be a resounding yes. "I like Nick. I love him...I think he's wonderful. But I married once before thinking I'd found The One, and I was tragically mistaken." She laughed, but it sounded bitter. "Life has a way of reminding you that you know nothing, doesn't it? Just when you hit adulthood and think you have it all figured out, a storm blows through and tears off your roof."

"That's one way of putting it." Dev was still resting his chin on his hands, watching her.

"I wanted to believe that being a doctor was my life. That being married to Jason Landish and raising children with him was my destiny. But neither of those things were true. So how do I know if what I believe right now, or yesterday, or tomorrow—how do I know if any of those things are true?"

Dev raised his eyebrows as she spoke.

"Do you know anything for a fact?" Lucy implored, setting down her knife and fork and leaning into the table so that their faces were inches closer. "What do you believe to be true, Dev?"

He sat back in his chair and let his hands rest on the table. "I know for a fact that I love my family. I know I believe in my business. I know I'm the kind of guy who means what he says and says what he means. I'm not the most polished or outgoing man you'll ever meet, but I believe that I have a good heart. I believe that I have feelings for you, and that I was willing to fly to freaking *Fiji*," he said, looking around at the beach incredulously, like he'd just been reminded of their surroundings, "to be with you. To tell you that I like you. And I know that was the right thing to do."

It was Lucy's turn to lean back in her chair. She blinked and looked at Dev. "Wow. You're very certain about what you believe."

"I don't second-guess myself much. No one knows me better than I do, so I figure, hey—if I don't trust my own feelings, no one else will."

"That's very wise."

"Okay, your turn. Just off the top of your head, what do you believe for yourself?" Dev lifted his chin at her.

Lucy exhaled and narrowed her eyes as she thought. "I believe I need to be a better daughter. I believe that leaving Buffalo and my career was the right choice for me at the time. I believe that opening a travel agency and seeing the world has changed me for the better already. I believe that just because I had my heart broken and my trust shattered, it doesn't mean that *I'm* broken and shattered. I believe I'm worthy of love, and that I have it to give." Lucy's eyes widened. "I had no idea I was going to say any of that."

Dev gave a low whistle. "Now we're getting somewhere."

"Alright, I see where this is going," Lucy said, looking at her plate. "My answers were pretty revealing. I'm still working on myself, and you're thinking that someone who doesn't have their own heart figured out probably shouldn't be trying to offer it to anyone else."

When she looked up, Dev was watching her. He shrugged lightly as they waited for their plates to be cleared. A second server appeared with two dishes of ice cream and two spoons, setting them down and backing away quietly.

"And to that I would say you're drawing your own conclusions, but I don't think they're entirely wrong."

Lucy picked up her spoon and scraped at the ice cream absent-mindedly. "Then I guess you know what I'm going to tell you."

Dev stared at her intently. "I think I do. But the real question is, what are you going to tell Nick?"

Chapter 18

July 5

Fiji

Mindy showed up at Kona's front door after dark with both dogs in tow. She took a minute before knocking, listening to the guitar music he was playing inside as he cooked, which she'd seen him doing through the uncurtained windows as she'd approached.

She lifted a hand and knocked twice. Kona threw open the door almost instantly, holding a spatula in one hand and wearing an enormous grin.

"Hi," he said, taking a step back to let her in with Bridger and Bagley. "And hello to you two," he said, looking at the dogs. "Glad you all could come."

Mindy set her small tote bag down by the door. She'd packed her toothbrush and a nightshirt along with a change of underwear, but had tried to disguise it all as an oversized purse in case Kona wasn't going to invite her to stay over. She still felt so hesitant about little things like that, even though he'd done nothing but treat her as though he was fascinated by everything she did and said. Absent from their interactions were the usual intricacies of dating, and completely missing was the dance that Mindy was accustomed to doing with men whereby she had to extrapolate from their behaviors and words whether they were interested in her, if they found her pleasing to the eye, and if they had any sort of designs on a long-term relationship.

With Kona, things were just easy. No doubt because she was leaving and therefore the pressure was off, but even setting that fact aside, things just felt more relaxed. He clearly thought she was beautiful, and at no point had she caught him assessing her and mentally tallying up the eventual costs of her physical maintenance to keep her presentable. All of a sudden it seemed like a shame to her that she and her other single female friends of a certain age had allowed themselves to be deemed worthy or unworthy based on whether or not they'd need a neck lift or breast implants in the next five years.

"You look stunning," Kona said, bending forward to kiss her lightly on the lips.

Mindy ran a hand through her loose hair. Since she'd started surfing with him in the mornings, she'd gotten into the habit of washing her hair after and just letting it dry in the sun. She hadn't blown it out even once during her time in Fiji, and she'd even stopped putting on her full face of makeup. After all, the sun had kissed her nose, her cheeks, and her temples, leaving her with a better glow than even the most expensive bronzer could provide.

"Thank you," Mindy said, closing the door behind her. "You don't look so bad yourself." And he didn't. He had on a light blue t-shirt that matched his eyes, and a pair of gray shorts. As he returned to the stove to stir whatever delicious smelling thing he was making, she got a clear view of his backside and his bare calves and feet. He was an extremely sexy man, and Mindy's eyes lingered while he worked.

"I hope you're staying over," Kona said without turning around. "Because I don't want to wake up tomorrow morning and find you gone. Now you don't have these guys as an excuse to escape." He waved his spatula in the general direction of her pups, who had, shockingly, found a spot they liked and immediately settled in without a peep.

"I'd love to stay," Mindy said, walking over to the couch in the open area. She kicked off her sandals and flopped down on it, pulling her feet up under her as she watched him cook. "I'd love to stay forever," she added, lowering her voice and hoping that he wouldn't hear it over the sizzle of vegetables and meat in the pan.

"I can't say I'd mind that too much," Kona said, surprising her. "Waking up and surfing with you everyday, having coffee, walking the dogs...that sounds pretty nice." He shut off the stove and removed the pan, carrying it over to the butcher block island and dumping the contents into a steel bowl.

"It sounds like the kind of life I dream of on cold winter mornings in New York," Mindy said, tugging at her earlobe as she leaned one elbow on the back of his couch. "Oh god," she said, swinging her legs around and putting her feet on the floor. "What am I doing being lazy here while you do all the cooking—tell me what to do to help."

Kona glanced her way with a smile. "You're all good, lady. I'm just making a simple dish of meat and veggies over rice with a sauce. Actually, there's a bottle of wine in the fridge. Do you want to open and pour?"

Within minutes, they had dinner laid out on his handmade table and they were seated, holding their wine glasses and looking at one another like they'd just won the lottery.

"How was the day?" Mindy asked, watching his muscled arms flex as he dished up their food.

"I gave a few lessons," Kona said, handing her a plate piled high with rice, different colored peppers, and ground beef. There was a dish of sauce in the middle of the table and he nodded at it, indicating that she should try some. "And now I'm having dinner here with you, so basically it was a perfect day."

"This whole trip has been perfect," Mindy said, taking her first bite. "I wasn't sure about going on vacation with a travel group, but honestly, it's been pretty low-key."

"Yeah, what's with that? You could have easily come to the resort on your own. Why'd you join a group?"

Mindy gave a one-shouldered shrug. "For being as old as I am, I have to tell you that I haven't really vacationed on my own all that many times. And it just felt...safer. Like I had someone who I could check in with. I know it sounds weird and I haven't really hung out with them much at all, but it's been nice to be a part of a group."

Kona nodded as he used an oversized spoon to put sauce on his rice. "And now that you've been here and loved it, do you think you'll come back?"

"I never want to leave," Mindy said honestly. "If I could just live in my bungalow and keep paying Dean to come and take my dogs out while I surf every morning, then I could be happy."

He was quiet for a minute. "Then you should stay."

Mindy nearly choked on her food. "Stay? Like, just move to Fiji for real?"

Kona gave her a long, serious look. "I'm not trying to be indelicate, Mindy, but don't you have the money? You could live anywhere you want on the island, and if you needed to go to your kids or bring them to you, I'm sure that would be something you could make happen."

Mindy was quiet as she ate. He wasn't wrong. But packing up her life and moving to another country where she'd been for less than a week was beyond impetuous. It wasn't crazy like, "Hey, maybe I should marry my ex-husband's brother" crazy, but it was definitely something she needed to give some thought to.

"I mean, I do love it here," she said, setting her fork on the edge of the plate. "But what are you suggesting in terms of us?"

Kona stood up and walked to the kitchen, riffling through his cabinet for something with his back to her. "I'm not sure yet," he said. "I don't want to go crazy here, I just know I like you. And you seem to like me." He closed the cupboard and turned around to face her. "I feel like if you leave here with no plans to come back, then this will have all been a dream. Or worse, a vacation fling."

145

"I would never want to be lumped together with your vacation flings," Mindy said firmly, feeling a lump grow in her throat at the thought that she might just be one of many for Kona.

In fact, maybe he had a new woman every week. Another sad, single woman traipsing around the resort like she'd just discovered the key to happiness and freedom, treating herself to a surfing lesson with a man who looked like he'd been carved from marble, and then falling into his bed in a bungalow hidden between the palm trees.

"Whatever it is you're thinking right now, you can just stop," Kona said, coming back to the table. "I can see it written all over your face. I'm not the guy you think I am, Mindy. I don't do 'vacation flings' with the women who frequent my family's resort. I just met you and I liked you, and it's as simple as that."

"I like you too," she said softly, picking up her fork again and pushing the rice around on her plate.

"I don't want to do anything crazy, you know? Like suggest you leave your life behind and move into my little house here. I don't want to ask you for things that are unreasonable at our age. I just want you to know that you have options. No one is forcing you to stay in New York if you aren't happy—are they?" He frowned. "Because if they are, I will fly there and have a word with them myself."

"No," Mindy said, laughing. "No one is forcing me. And yes, I have all the money I could ever need or want, so nothing is out of the realm of possibility." She stopped talking and let her mind wander. Moving her life to the South Pacific: good idea, or totally misguided attempt at plastering over a midlife crisis? It would be nothing for her to give up her places on the various committees and charities she served on, and to sell off her apartment and belongings. Or, hell, rent it all out. Give it to her children. Give it to Lalo, her doorman of fifteen years. Maybe he could move his wife Gloria and their kids into her apartment and breathe new life into the old place. Her kids would die if she did that, and just the thought of it brought a smile to her face.

"What are you thinking about?" Kona asked, spooning more food onto his plate from the serving dish in the center of the table. "You're smiling."

"You know," Mindy said, feeling herself relax as realization dawned over her. "I *can* do anything I want. I'm a free woman. I have no one who counts on me every day, and I can live my life as I see fit. That's totally liberating. And until I came here, I'm not sure I truly believed that. But having my son call me out on how I choose to donate my money and realizing that my financial advisor is a misogynistic asshole who calls my son instead of me when he has a question about my money really drove home the fact that I don't need them. I don't need my daughters nitpicking my life choices every single day, and I don't need the life I have in New York to give me purpose."

Kona's brow furrowed as he listened.

"And even though it makes no sense, I have you to thank for all of that. You helped me stand up on a surfboard and catch my first wave. You look at me like you think I'm beautiful."

"I do think you're beautiful."

"Thank you." Mindy smiled. "And I needed all of that."

"But?"

She closed her eyes and squeezed them shut. "But I don't know. I'm not sure I'm ready to give up New York. My whole life has been there, and I didn't come here wanting to never return." She opened her eyes and looked straight at him. "Finding the place that feels like home is a big deal."

"It is," he agreed mildly, still watching her.

"And yet...I hesitate to even say this for fear of sounding like one of those wacky people who goes on vacation and decides to quit their job and move there, but Fiji feels like home too."

Kona's face melted into a huge grin. "So you'll stay?" he asked hopefully.

"I'll postpone going home, but only if you promise to show me the rest of the island immediately. I want to see it all and figure out where and how I might live."

"Immediately?" Kona asked, one side of his mouth tugging up at the corner. "Do you think it could wait until tomorrow?"

Mindy threw her head back and laughed. "Oh? You have other plans for this evening?"

Kona was out of his chair so fast that Bridger and Bagley didn't even have a chance to jump up from the floor and bark with excitement. He picked Mindy up out of her seat and carried her across the big, open space, making a beeline for his bed.

"I do have other plans for this evening," he said, tossing her onto the white duvet and making her laugh even harder. "You wanna sleep over?"

"I do want to stay over, but no one ever said anything about sleeping," Mindy said, reaching up and grabbing the hem of his blue t-shirt and tugging it. "Come here."

Kona pulled the shirt over his head and knelt on the foot of the bed, watching Mindy's face as he lowered himself over her and put his lips to hers. "I'm here," he said, nuzzling her nose with his as he kissed her again. "I'm here, Mindy."

Chapter 19

July 6

Fiji

The trip was almost over and Lucy knew what had to be done. She woke up early on the last full day of their time in Fiji, ready to face the music.

Nick, for his part, had continued to sleep on the couch in her bungalow, and was still fast asleep, one arm flung over his eyes to block out the morning sun. Lucy tiptoed past him and closed the door to the bathroom, where she quietly showered and dressed and packed up the things that she'd spread all around over the past week.

When she came out, Nick had rolled over and was on his stomach. Instead of waking him, she sent a text to both him and Dev telling them to meet her at the smallest pool on the property, where she knew from walking past it each morning that she'd find peace and quiet, as most families gravitated toward the big pool with the slides or the infinity pool.

Lucy stopped at one of the restaurants for a cup of coffee first, and when she got to the pool she chose three chairs, pulling them closer together under the shady palm trees. She kicked off her sandals and sat, watching the water as it rippled in the morning breeze. She had about thirty minutes alone before Dev showed up, holding his own coffee.

"Morning, Miss Adventure," he said, letting himself in through the gate. He took the chair on her left, looking grim and determined.

"Hi," Lucy said, lifting her coffee in greeting.

They sat together in silent contemplation for another ten minutes until Nick showed up, hair still wet from a shower. He looked stressed as he walked up to the pool gate with a towel under one arm and his sunglasses on top of his head. A pang of hurt ricocheted through Lucy as she realized that he was the kindest, most caring, honest man she'd known in years and she was about to hurt him.

"Oh," Nick said, dropping his towel onto the other chair and sitting. "I guess we're not here for a morning swim."

Lucy sat up and set her coffee on the ground so that she could put both hands in her lap. She looked back and forth between these two men—these two wonderful men—who had come all the way from Florida in hopes of winning or keeping her heart. For a moment, her chin dropped and she stared at her hands.

"So," she said, breaking the silence. "Today is the last day of this trip, and having you both here has been eye-opening. I've really been forced to look at some things."

"Let's stay longer," Nick blurted out. "I don't even care if it's all three of us," he said, sweeping a hand dismissively in Dev's direction. "I just want more time. You need to understand how committed I am to making this work."

"Nick," Lucy said softly, reaching over and taking his hand in hers. "I've never known anyone more committed to making something work. You're amazing."

He nodded slowly. "I sense a 'but' in there somewhere."

"The only 'but' is me," Lucy said, turning to look at Dev as well. "I've done some real soul searching here on Fiji, and I really think I'm not done picking up my own pieces. And until I am, all I can offer is a half-finished puzzle—to either of you. Or to anyone else. And that's not fair."

"But don't you think sometimes the missing pieces to your puzzle are the ones that someone else brings to the table?" Nick asked.

Lucy nodded, thinking about it. "To a certain extent. But there are some things in a person that have to be whole. I'm over my ex-husband, but guys, I'm not over my divorce. I'm not over the way it all ended. That rattles your cage in a way that's hard to comprehend. I've also got some real complications in my life at the moment: legal entanglements with the ex in question, and some heavy lifting with my mother that's only going to get heavier. I need to work through those things. Sand over the rough edges. Figure out how to be me and still be what other people need me to be."

Dev spoke up for the first time. "I don't like it," he said, clearing his throat, "but I understand it. I know I came here and really shook things up for you, and I won't lie and say that wasn't my intention, but I certainly didn't want you to go back into your shell and be all alone."

Lucy looked at Dev and then back at Nick. "I'm not alone," she said, smiling for the first time since they'd sat down. "If you two will have me, then we're still in each other's lives. And I can't ask you to wait while I get my life and my heart together, but I do think that time will cause things to unfold, and who knows what that will look like. For any of us."

"I'm pretty stunned," Nick said, eyes wide as he stared at the concrete pool deck. Just then, an extremely tanned older man with a potbelly and three layers of gold chains around his neck let himself into the pool and coughed loudly as he chose a chair far away from them. "I never thought I'd come here and lose you."

"You're not losing me," Lucy said imploringly, looking at Nick's face even though he wouldn't make eye contact with her. "I just need to find me. Let me put myself together before I try to hand over part of my heart to anyone. I'm sorry, Nick, this isn't what I wanted, but it is what feels right at the moment."

Dev stood up. "I'm gonna leave you two," he said carefully,

holding up a hand. "Thanks for your honesty, Lucy." He took his coffee and walked away, letting the pool gate clink shut behind him.

Nick finally looked at her, and there was a fire in his eyes Lucy had never seen before. "Are you breaking things off with me because you want to be with Dev?" he asked, his voice full of unmasked hurt.

"No," she said honestly, shaking her head so firmly that her hair swung back and forth. "I'm being completely straightforward here."

Nick looked up at the sky. "So you really want to be on your own right now?"

"I think I need to be. You and I have something that I'm afraid to lose, but I'm more afraid to lose myself. To spread myself too thin so that I'm doing a ton of things, but none of them particularly well."

Nick nodded and rested his elbows on his knees. "Okay," he said. "Okay."

Lucy leaned over and put a hand on Nick's warm back, rubbing what she hoped were soothing circles over his cotton t-shirt.

"Can you just give me that?" she asked softly. "Can you give me some time? That's all I'm asking for."

Nick looked like he'd been slapped in the face. "I can give you time, Lucy, but I'm pretty pissed—I can't lie about that. Dev comes down here and all of a sudden you're not my girl anymore. That sucks."

"I know, but it's not because of him," she said, leaning in even closer. "It's because of me."

"You make me so happy, Lucy," he said, his voice catching. "And when we were on South Sea Island yesterday, I really thought you were happy too. Like, big picture happy, not just in that moment."

"And I am," she said, trying to find the words to explain it, "but I'm also not. I'm happy with you, but I'm not happy with me. Not yet, anyway."

Nick breathed in and out and then pushed himself to his feet. "Okay," he said, looking down at her and holding her gaze for a long moment. "I hear what you're saying. And like Dev said, I guess thank you for being up front. Better to hear this now than later, although hearing it on an island 7,000 miles from home is pretty brutal. The flight back will give me too much time to think."

"Nick..." Lucy said, looking up at him as he stood there.

"Listen, I'll see you back at home," he said, shoving both hands into his pockets. "Take care, Lucy." And then he left.

Lucy sat there for several minutes, wondering if by "see you back home" he meant that he'd meet her in the bungalow and they'd find their way to the airport together the next morning, or if he'd meant that he'd see her back on Amelia Island.

But when she got back to her bungalow later, every sign of Nick had been erased as if he'd never been there, and Lucy knew then what he'd meant.

She spent the last twenty-four hours of her time in Fiji on her own, smiling hollowly (but convincingly) at her tour group as she bid them all farewell and safe travels, and then she flew home alone, face turned to the window as she watched the water and the mountains and the earth below.

Chapter 20

July 12

Fiji

Spencer examined her cuticles while she waited for hair and makeup to work their magic on the women who were going to be seated at the bar for this shot. She'd been working hard on editing her footage in every spare second she had, but Heinrich had been clear that he needed her to do her real job during the times she was expected to be on set, and so she was trying her best to help wrap up this season of *Wild Tropics* and make it as good as it could be.

The majority of the Holiday Adventure Club group had vanished several days ago like a wave receding on the beach, but Spencer had seen Mindy Shultz still roaming the grounds of the resort with her two dogs, or sitting in the grass next to the hot surf instructor guy. It seemed as though she'd taken up permanent residence at the Frangipani Fiji, which tickled Spencer to no end. Because her parents ran in the same circles as the Shultzes back home, she knew what Mindy was missing, and she was honestly happy for her that she'd decided to stay in paradise rather than head back home to the steamy, crowded streets of Manhattan to brave the traffic for Instagram-worthy weekends in the Hamptons. She knew from talking to her mother that there was a huge Lincoln Center fundraiser meant to reinvigorate the performing arts post-pandemic coming up that Mindy would have been expected to attend, full of fussy middle-aged people in tuxedoes and expensive gowns, and that boozy, gossipy lunches at The Mary Lane, La Parisienne, and Amélie would have been on Mindy's agenda.

But this was so much better. Seeing Mindy with her hair unstyled, comfortable in shorts and sandals, and letting her dogs chase one another on the beach or the grass was refreshing. It gave Spencer hope that her own future could be whatever she wanted it to be, and not some pre-prescribed cookie cutter life that had suited her mother and her friends but would never be right for her.

"Spence?" Todd said, walking over to her with a light meter in one hand and a cell phone in the other. "Call for you."

He handed her the phone and she looked at the screen. Across the bar, Heinrich had his arms folded and he was frowning as he listened to another crew member talking intently. He really was a handsome man, Spencer thought; handsome and kind and funny, and she wasn't sure why he seemed to insecure in their relationship. She liked him, and she wanted him to accept that at face value. There didn't have to be anything more than that at the moment.

"Hello?" she said, putting the phone to her ear.

"Hi, Spencer, Bill Pullman here."

Spencer's spine straightened automatically. Bill Pullman was big time. He was someone who could make or break her career if she chose to stay at the network. He was also the one who'd let Heinrich know that she'd gone slightly rogue while working on *Wild Tropics*, so she answered guardedly.

"Hello, Bill. Thank you for calling," she said, anticipating that he would be wanting to discuss the rough cut of her footage she'd sent his way.

Bill gave what sounded like an amused chuckle. "Sure thing," he said. "I've watched what you sent, and I have to say, I'm intrigued."

Spencer felt a thrill run through her. "Oh!" she said, waiting for him to go on.

"I'm entertained that Heinrich has allowed you to do your own thing, but I'm also impressed, because sometimes we don't give people room to run wild with their creativity, and he's clearly encouraged that here. You've got some solid footage."

"Thank you," Spencer said, beaming. She looked in Heinrich's direction again and he smiled at her, giving her a wink.

"So here's my thought," Bill Pullman said, pushing ahead. "I'd like to see the rest of what you got, and I'll need confirmation of signed releases from everyone you followed. We can't use any of this if the people on camera haven't given their express permission."

"Okay, got it," Spencer said, knowing that she had what he needed. Everyone she'd followed had been totally fine signing release forms. "And what do you ultimately see happening with the footage? It doesn't really play into this season of *Wild Tropics*, which I knew going into it, but I thought there was a real story to tell. Several stories to tell, to be honest."

"Agreed," Bill said. "What I'd like to do is get the footage edited into something that looks a bit less polished. I want to put it up on the website as a kind of 'behind the scenes at the resort' sort of thing. Bonus footage. Kind of a docudrama. A look at the real people and the real lives there. I don't have a name for it yet, but I think there'll be a certain segment of the viewers who are interested enough to click and watch this sort of thing."

"I agree, Bill," Spencer said, trying to hold herself together and not melt down from the excitement that was buzzing through her and causing her hands to shake. "I think that sounds incredible."

Bill laughed generously. "I bet you do. Anyhow, I wanted to give you the good news myself, and to tell you that I really admire that sort of out-of-the-box thinking, Spencer. Keep doing good work down there, and I'll be in touch."

"Thank you so much," she said, clinging to her calm façade by the last threads as they ended the call.

"Heinz!" she shouted, jumping up and down and waving her arms back and forth to get Heinrich's attention. "Heinz!"

Heinrich stopped what he was doing and turned to look at Spencer as she raced across the bar and threw her arms wide. She wrapped them around his neck as she laughed with joy.

"Bill Pullman said he liked what I had! He said they could use it, and he admired my creativity!"

"I know," Heinrich said into her ear, hugging her. "I know."

Spencer pulled back and looked into his eyes. "Are you okay with this?"

Heinrich looked at her and his eyes didn't stray from her face. "With..."

"Are you okay with me submitting my footage and doing all of this when I was supposed to be assisting full-time?"

He gave her a half-smile. "Yeah, I'm okay with it. I would never want to stand in the way of someone's budding career."

Spencer looked around at the rest of the cast; half of them were still working on whatever they'd been doing, paying little or no attention to the boss getting hugged by an assistant. The other half were watching but pretending not to.

Heinrich was still looking at her.

"And are you okay with this?" Spencer asked, taking a hesitant step closer to him so that their chests were just inches apart. "And maybe this?" she said, lacing her fingers through his. Heinrich didn't look away from her, but she could see his neck redden and his ears turn pink as his eyes questioned her. "And also this," Spencer said, dropping her voice as she stood on her toes and turned her chin up to kiss him.

Heinrich kissed her back, hesitantly at first, but to his credit, he didn't move away. Spencer looped her arms around his neck again and kept kissing him, letting her eyes close as she lost herself in the moment. Heinrich's arms went around her and held her tight; she could feel his lips curve into a smile under hers.

"So you are okay with this?" she asked, pulling her mouth away just an inch and looking into his eyes. "You're okay with everyone officially knowing about us? Because you know they already know *un*officially."

Heinrich looked around at the cast and crew, and now every set of eyes was on them. "Are you okay with it?" he asked, glancing at her face.

"Hell yeah, I am," Spencer said, putting her lips to his one more time. "I'm totally okay with it. I like you, Heinrich. I really like you."

As they kissed again, their future not mapped out or set in stone, but at least out in the open, boldly and honestly, everyone in the bar burst into applause and loud cheers and whistles.

Chapter 21

July 31

St. Louis, MO

Lucy sat in the same mediation room in the same courthouse as the same air-conditioning unit struggled to keep everyone from dying of a heatstroke. She fanned herself with a folder and wished she was on Amelia Island so that she could at least race to the beach and throw herself into the ocean for some relief from the humidity. Instead, she was stuck inside, bugs swarming around everywhere outside, watching her ex-husband once again across the table as their lawyers made suggestions and hemmed and hawed over details.

"I'll give up the portion of the inheritance that gives me control," Lucy said suddenly, not even realizing that she was about to speak. "Half is fine. I don't need to be able to have the final say in everything."

Lucy's lawyer turned to look at her incredulously. "Lucy," Nelson Bunch, her second attorney, said. "By giving up the right to veto Mr. Landish on any business-related matters, you are essentially saying that you're willing to negotiate with him going forward each time you two have something you want to do with the property."

"No," Lucy said, setting down the folder she'd been fanning

herself with. "I don't want that. But I am willing to allow him to buy me out at fifty percent of the market value. Then he can do what he wants with the property and we won't need to ever do *this* again." She waved a hand at the room.

Jason's lawyer, Axel Pleury, turned his wedding band nervously on his finger as he frowned. "Mr. Landish, is this something you're willing to consider?"

Jason looked puzzled. He'd clearly been expecting Lucy to battle him until the end of time over every detail of these properties, and now she'd made an offer that would effectively end any communication between them. With the buyout, they would never need to speak to one another again unless they wanted to.

"I'll need to talk to my wife," he said, "and I'm inclined to negotiate. Would Lucy be willing to accept a buyout at thirty percent?"

Lucy huffed. "No way."

"Forty?" Jason's eyebrows shot up expectantly.

Lucy leaned over and whispered something to Nelson Bunch, then stood up, gathering her folder and her purse. She didn't bother to look at Jason as she walked across the hot room, her heels clicking against the wood floors. As she walked out, she could hear her attorney speaking, but she didn't slow down or turn back.

"Mrs. Landish is willing to sell at forty-five percent and not a point lower. I can have the papers drawn up today if you're both willing to sign while she's still in town, and then you can go on and start figuring out the financials of the deal..." Nelson's words trailed off as Lucy walked down the hallway, head held high.

Sure, she'd take forty-five percent. It was forty-five percent of money that she never even thought she'd have, and it would only serve to help her as she paved her way forward in life. She'd take forty-five percent of what Marion Landish had sent her way in death like the cantankerous, ballsy angel she'd always been in life. And deep down, she knew Marion would be proud and not disappointed, because a woman had to do what a woman had to do to get by.

Lucy pushed open the courthouse doors and a wave of midsummer humidity hit her like a fog. She was going home to Florida and to the beach and to her bungalow, and then she was going to pack her bags and head to Lisbon in September, because the whole world was just out there waiting.

The whole world was out there, and Lucy was ready to find her place in it.

Ready for the next book in the Holiday Adventure Club Series?

Join the Holiday Adventure Club as they take a trip to Lisbon for Labor Day. Buy it today from your favorite bookstore here!

About the Author

Stephanie Taylor is a high-school teacher who loves sushi, "The Golden Girls," Depeche Mode, orchids, and coffee. She is the author of the Christmas Key books, a romantic comedy series about a fictional island off the coast of Florida, as well as The Holiday Adventure Club series.

https://redbirdsandrabbits.com
    redbirdsandrabbits@gmail.com

Also by Stephanie Taylor

Stephanie also writes a long-running romantic comedy series set on a fictional key off the coast of Florida. Christmas Key is a magical place that's decorated for the holidays all year round, and you'll instantly fall in love with the island and its locals.

To see a complete list of the Christmas Key series along with all of Stephanie's other books, please visit:

Stephanie Taylor's Books

To hear about any new releases, sign up here and you'll be the first to know!

Made in the USA
Columbia, SC
05 March 2024

32682615R00093